JENNIFER COLLINS JOHNSON

Arizona Cowboy

HEARTSONG
PRESENTS

Recycling programs
for this product may
not exist in your area.

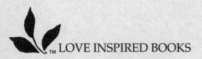

TM LOVE INSPIRED BOOKS

ISBN-13: 978-0-373-48726-4

ARIZONA COWBOY

www.Harlequin.com

Printed in U.S.A.

The Lord is close to the brokenhearted
and saves those who are crushed in spirit.
—*Psalms* 34:18

Writers must find a balance between heartbreak and victory. We must be honest with the true deep-to-the-core pain our characters feel when they face tragedy, and yet, as a Christian writer, I want to always show that no matter the hardship, God can heal us and make us victors if we allow. Ava and Holden's challenges ripped at my heart, and I dedicate this book to anyone who has ever endured their loss. May each of you find peace and comfort in Him.

The Lord is close to the brokenhearted
and saves those who are crushed in spirit.
—*Psalms* 34:18

Writers must find a balance between heartbreak and victory. We must be honest with the true deep-to-the-core pain our characters feel when they face tragedy, and yet, as a Christian writer, I want to always show that no matter the hardship, God can heal us and make us victors if we allow. Ava and Holden's challenges ripped at my heart, and I dedicate this book to anyone who has ever endured their loss. May each of you find peace and comfort in Him.

Chapter 1

Ava Herbert twisted the gray and black crepe paper together, then taped the streamers to the corner of her aunt's smooth yellow ceiling. She smiled at the color contrast. Most people mourned birthdays, especially ones that ushered in a new decade. Not Aunt Irene. She embraced each day with laughter and sunshine.

"You know what Picasso said about birthdays," Aunt Irene had announced earlier that afternoon, while Ava's cousin, Mitch, tried to prod his mother out the door so Ava could decorate in secret.

Ava and her cousins had planned a surprise party for her aunt's sixtieth birthday, but keeping a secret from the ever-nosy woman had been more of a challenge than any of them anticipated.

"What did Picasso say?" Ava had responded.

Aunt Irene winked. "He said it takes a long time to become young."

"I don't know that I agree," Mitch had muttered as he'd

stood at the front door, the warm March sun shining through the glass. The temperature was actually mild for Surprise, Arizona—only seventy-two degrees. "I can feel gray hairs growing as I wait on my mother to exit the house."

"Oh hush." Aunt Irene had swatted his arm as they'd finally walked out the door.

Aunt Irene's sons were as much of a contrast to their mother as the dark streamers were to the sunny ceiling paint. Both of them were grumpy and literal-thinking men.

Now Ava and Mitch's brother, Matt, were finally able to decorate in peace. She stepped off the dining room chair and knelt on the table, below the ceiling fan Aunt Irene had painted bright orange, with yellow Indian mallow flowers on the blades. "Hand me those balloons, will ya, Matt?"

"Sure."

Ava took them from him and taped them to the center of the fan, then jumped off the table to survey her work. Crepe paper hung in four lines from the walls around the table. The streamers joined in the center, with black and gray balloons hanging from the fan. Matt had taped a Happy Birthday banner on one wall. Smiling skeletons peeked from behind tombstones on both sides.

Ava clapped. "What do ya think?"

Matt shrugged. "Looks fine, I guess."

She punched his arm. "No wonder you still don't have a girlfriend. You're supposed to say it looks fantastic."

He rolled his eyes. "I've made it through thirty-five years without a wife. I can wait a little longer. If God wants me to marry, then…"

"I know, cuz. I was just kidding."

"God has a plan, Ava. I don't have to run around, worrying over women…."

She rose on tiptoe and kissed her six-foot-tall cousin's

cheek. "I promise I was teasing. Will you get the fruit and veggies out of the refrigerator in the garage?"

Ava watched as Matt walked away. Her cousin was a wonderful man of faith. He worked tirelessly for home missions in Arizona, and would make a terrific husband, but the poor guy had absolutely no sense of humor.

She glanced at the enormous brass wall clock behind the dining room table. Mitch was probably about to pick up Aunt Irene's best friend. From there, he'd talk his mom into stopping by a restaurant for a quick dinner, which meant Ava had a little over an hour before Irene got home, but only thirty minutes until guests arrived.

Racing into the spare bedroom, she felt her heart skip, as it did each time she stepped into the room. The last time Ava lived with her aunt had been the summer she'd fallen in love with a local cattle rancher, Holden Whitaker. Her aunt hadn't changed anything in the bedroom, and now that Ava had moved back in until she could find her own place, she found herself overcome with memories each time she entered.

"He never even came in here," she muttered as she made her way toward the mission-style dresser. The sage-colored walls still held a mixture of Native American and Mexican memorabilia from her aunt's many travels to Mexico, Texas and Oklahoma. Ava flattened a wrinkle in the multicolored patchwork quilt. *But I spent many a night in this room dreaming of him.*

She turned to the dresser, opened the bottom drawer and searched for a pair of light khaki capris. Her fingertip touched the edge of the snapshot of herself and Holden. She didn't have to look at it; the picture was etched in her mind. When she'd moved back in with Aunt Irene, Ava had found it taped to the mirror above the dresser, exactly where she'd left it. Unable to leave it on display like that, with the love-filled couple smiling at her every day, she'd stowed the photo in the bureau drawer, since she couldn't get rid of it, either. Lifting the picture out now, she looked at it, really looked at it, for the first time since she'd returned.

A younger Ava faced the camera with a big, cheesy grin. Her hair, long and really blond, fell down both shoulders. Her complexion was white, so white compared to Holden's sun-kissed skin. But it wasn't the image of her that punctured Ava's heart. In the picture, Holden stared down at her. His oversize cowboy hat and the fact that his face was in profile made it impossible to see his smoky blue eyes. But she didn't have to see them; even now she could feel them. Could feel his strong arm wrapped around her shoulder. Her Arizona cowboy, she'd called him. He'd loved her with a force she couldn't comprehend at the age of eighteen. A force she still feared eight years later.

His heart had been steadfast in the Lord. His faith so strong. He'd been confident they would make it, even though they were only twenty and eighteen years old at the time. She knew he wanted to marry her, and maybe if they'd waited... Ava shook the thought away. She hadn't been ready for the seriousness of their relationship. It scared her, and she'd panicked.

Her heart beat faster at the memory. Her palms grew clammy.

She'd quickly written him a letter, gently kissed his upturned lips as he slept, then ran. He'd tried to contact her. Through Aunt Irene. Her parents. Even Mitch and Matt. He'd begged to talk with her. Had apologized. But she ignored him. Within a few weeks, she'd moved away to college and shoved the memory of him to the farthest recesses of her mind. For several months, anyway.

She touched the brim of his hat in the picture. *I wish*

I hadn't been so afraid, Lord. He would have supported me through college. He would have helped me through...

No. She shook her head. She would not allow her thoughts to take that path. Not today. It was Aunt Irene's day, and Ava couldn't change the past.

She placed the picture at the bottom of the drawer again. After finding her capris, she slipped into them, changed into her favorite aqua blouse and accented the outfit with a coral bracelet, necklace and earrings. She brushed through her layered highlights, then reapplied her coral lipstick.

Her smartphone beeped, announcing a new text message. She opened it. Mom and Dad wouldn't be able to make Irene's surprise party. Ava sent a quick "that's fine" message back.

It was no surprise her dad couldn't make his sister's six-tieth birthday party. He and her mom acknowledged Ava's own birthday with only a card, filled with cash, of course. Business. Her parents were always busy with business.

She shoved the phone into her front pocket and opened the bedroom door. Two of Irene's neighbors had already arrived. Ava pushed all thoughts of Holden and of her mom and dad to the back of her mind. *Today is for one of the most amazing women I've ever known. Aunt Irene.*

Holden Whitaker gripped the steering wheel of his new maroon F-150. He hadn't planned to attend Irene's party, hadn't even known anything about it. But when he ran into Mitch and Irene at the restaurant, and Irene had been so happy to see him, and Mitch took Holden aside and told him about the surprise birthday party Ava was throwing... Holden twisted the rubber on the wheel and swallowed back his nerves. He just couldn't tell Mitch no. Irene had always been so good to Holden and his sisters after their mom died. His acceptance to the surprise party had nothing to do with Ava. Nothing at all.

"Ava's spent the last two days getting ready...." Mitch's words replayed in his mind.

Holden wiped perspiration from his forehead with the back of his hand, then turned up the air conditioner in the truck. He'd gone on plenty of dates since Ava literally ran off on him eight years ago. Even tried to get serious with a couple of gals. His heartbeat raced, but there was something about that tiny blond-haired, blue-eyed firecracker that lit a fuse in his gut every time he thought about her. *Settle your nerves, Whitaker. You're not some twenty-year-old, moon-eyed pup anymore.*

To allow Mitch plenty of time to get his mom and her friend home, Holden stopped at the florist and picked up a bouquet of flowers for Irene's birthday. The temptation to buy Ava a bouquet of wildflowers, maybe some purple lupines and yellow poppies, since they were her favorite, nearly overwhelmed him, but he resisted.

Memories of Ava sitting beside him in his old brown work truck washed over him. If he focused, he could still smell her perfume. Well, almost. He turned onto Irene's street and saw Mitch pulling into the driveway. Holden tried to drive by, so as not to ruin the surprise, but Irene saw him and motioned for him to park behind them.

Feeling like a complete spoiler, Holden pulled into the driveway. Before he could open the door, Irene popped her head in the passenger's window. She scooped the bouquet off the seat. "These for me?"

"Yeah."

She smiled. "They're nice. Come on. I can't wait to see the look on Ava's face when she yells 'surprise' and then spies you."

Mitch frowned. "Mom, how did you know this was a surprise party?"

Irene motioned toward her friend. "Phoebe told me."

Holden glanced at the small woman with short brown hair. She shook her pointer finger back and forth in front of her face. "I told Ava not to tell me. I told her I couldn't keep a secret if my life depended on it. I made it a full day before Irene tricked me."

"I tricked you?" Irene chuckled. "I asked you what we should do for my birthday, and you spilled the beans."

"See?" Phoebe pointed toward Irene. "She tricked me."

"Well, I'm glad you didn't tell Ava. She's worked really hard." Mitch wrapped his arm around his mom's and guided her toward the door. "Act surprised."

Irene reached for Holden, grabbing the elbow of his long-sleeved brown shirt. "I will." She winked at him as she shoved him toward her friend. "Mitch and I will go through the door first. I want you two right behind us."

Phoebe grasped Holden's elbow. "I don't mean to tell secrets. It just happens." She peered up at him. "And it's not like I'm not completely honest with people. I tell them. Don't tell me anything you don't want shared."

Holden ignored the woman's musings as he imagined seeing Ava again for the first time in eight years. A sudden realization dawned on him. She could have a boyfriend, or worse yet, a fiancé, even a husband. She could have a child. Holden's stomach knotted. *Surely not.*

Irene flung open the door. Shouts of "surprise" echoed through the air. Before he could put two thoughts together, Phoebe dragged him through the entranceway. The first face he saw was Ava's.

In a moment, he drank in the sight of her. The short pants hugged her slender curves. The light blue shirt, though modest, dipped just far enough to remind him of the softness of her nape. Her blond hair was now cut in layers that framed her face and fell just below her shoulders.

Her eyebrows lifted in surprise and Holden drank in her ocean-blue eyes. Her complexion, clear and white, suddenly blanched, as one word seeped through her perfect, coral lips. "Holden."

Then she crumpled to the floor.

A cool softness caressed her forehead, then her cheeks, then her forehead again. Ava opened her eyes to a vision of stormy blue eyes peering at her with an intensity that squeezed her gut. Her gaze traveled down the straight nose to the perfect mixture of soft yet coarse, firm yet gentle lips. The deep dimple in the center of the chin gave the strong jawline just a touch of boyish charm. Ava placed her palm flat against the cheek. "Still beautiful."

The storm in his eyes deepened. His lips parted. "I'd say so."

Ava blinked. She blinked again. *I'm not dreaming.* She sat up. A wet rag fell from her face. She picked it up off her lap. *Oh, dear Lord, I'm not dreaming.* She looked past the figure of her dream and noted the dozen or more of Aunt Irene's friends, standing there. Her gaze stopped on her aunt, whose expression shifted from fear to knowing. Ava looked back at Holden.

Embarrassment crept up her neck as she realized what had happened. She started to stand, and a flash of dizziness swept through her head. Holden reached to help her, but she shook away the offer. "I'm okay." She dusted the back of her capris. "I'm okay. Just haven't eaten enough today, I guess." She chuckled, praying the guests would shift their attention away from her.

"I think my niece is fine now." Aunt Irene clapped. "Let's eat some of these goodies she's prepared."

The group started talking and moved toward the kitchen. Ava exhaled in relief, then realized Holden hadn't moved from her side. She swallowed the knot in her throat. She couldn't look at him.

A hand tugged her arm, and Ava turned toward her aunt. Concern etched Irene's features. "What have you eaten today?"

Ava dipped her chin. "Couple crackers. Few bites of banana."

"I want you to get yourself in that kitchen and fix a plate."

"I will."

Her aunt's expression softened. "You sure you're okay?"

Ava nodded. "Just surprised." She sneaked a quick peek at Holden, who was still beside her. He stared at her with an intensity that did nothing to aid her light-headedness. She turned to her aunt. "I'll be in the kitchen in a minute."

Irene nodded, then looked at Holden. She reached up and pinched his cheek. "It's good to see you, youngun'." She glanced back at Ava and winked, then walked toward her party guests.

Ava studied the new tile on the floor, fully aware of Holden's gaze boring into her. Her knees started to shake, so she shifted her weight from one foot to the other. Her hands trembled, and she clasped them together.

Holden touched her elbow and fire shot through her veins. "Let's get you some food."

"Wait." She gazed into his eyes, then looked away. "I'm sorry, Holden."

"Why'd you run?"

His question was direct and stern, just as Ava had imagined. She couldn't look at him again. She shrugged.

"That's not an answer."

With both hands, Holden gripped her arms, and she looked up at him. The pain in his eyes made her breath catch, and she bit her bottom lip. He lightened his touch. "Why, Ava?"

She pulled away from him and smacked her palm against her thigh. "Scared, I guess." She shrugged again and shook her head as she peered at him. "We were so young, Holden."

"I wanted to marry you."

Ava swallowed and looked away from him. Still a straight shooter. Said exactly what he thought. She straightened the afghan draped over the easy chair. "I know."

Holden moved close. She sucked in her breath as he gently touched her chin and lifted her face toward him. "I loved you."

"Ava?" Mitch's voice came from the hall. He stepped into the living room, then ducked his head. "Sorry, but they're ready to cut the cake."

Ava pulled away from Holden. Though her insides trembled, she plastered a smile on her lips. "The cake. Of course."

She took a step away. He grabbed her arm, and she looked back at him. "We're going to talk. I won't let you get away this time," he stated.

Pain laced through her. *Once you find out the truth, you will.*

Chapter 2

Ava took a deep breath as she pulled into the parking lot of Miller Physical Therapy Clinic. The contemporary-style building boasted all windows and a sleek glass door in front. Several of Arizona's hardier bushes and cacti bedded in ornate gravel lined the front of the business. She stepped out of the air-conditioned car, and the hot air encouraged the butterflies in her stomach to flutter faster. Lifting her purse strap higher on her shoulder, she made her way to the door, then gasped when she read the names of the therapists etched into the glass. *They've already added my name.*

She touched the letters. Her first real job since she finished her degree. She wouldn't start seeing patients on her own for another week, and yet they'd already added her name. Excitement welled within her as she pushed open the door. She smiled at the petite brunette sitting behind the reception desk. "Hi, Katie."

Katie popped her gum and motioned Ava through the door leading to the back. "Mom's waiting for you. Room 2."

"Thanks. How are your classes going?"

The young woman groaned. "Why'd you have to say that? My anatomy class is gonna kill me." She leaned closer to Ava and pointed toward the back rooms. "And if I don't do well, they're gonna kill me, too."

Ava laughed. "They will not. You've got the best parents in the world."

Katie popped her chewing gum again. "Not if I flunk that class."

"Then don't flunk."

"Don't flunk." Katie moved a pile of papers from one side of the desk to the other. "Don't flunk, she says. Do you know how many of my friends have had to drop that class? It's known as the weed-out class."

"You can do it." Ava tapped her hand before heading back to room 2. The girl was a bit on the flighty side, but she was young, only nineteen. Katie still had a lot of growing up to do. *Just as I did. I was even younger when I met Holden.* Ava knocked on the door.

"Come on in," Mary Miller called.

Ava walked inside and smiled at the older version of Katie, who still looked young and vibrant. No one would ever guess the brown-eyed brunette had a nineteen-year-old daughter and fourteen-year-old twin sons. Ava nodded at the older gentleman who stood behind a straight-back chair.

"Ava Herbert, this is Clyde Watkins. He's one of our regulars." Mary nudged the man's arm.

"Humph," the man growled. "You'd think with all the money I've put into therapy, Mary here would find a way to fix my arthritis. I think she just likes seeing me." A smile turned up his lips.

"Well, Clyde, you're going to be seeing a lot of Ava, as well. She's our new therapist."

"Really?" His eyebrows rose. "Then maybe I don't want to be fixed."

Mary laughed, and Ava couldn't help but join her. Then the older woman shook her head. "Clyde, you are such a flirt. I'm telling your wife."

"Go ahead and tell her. You and I both know why she likes to see that young buck of a husband of yours."

"I heard that."

Ava jumped at the sound of a voice behind her. She turned, spying a silver-haired woman sitting in a chair to the side of the door, her eyes twinkling. "Don't mind him, honey. We just like to tease the Millers."

Ava nodded, then watched intently while Mary finished the session with Clyde. She smiled at the sweet relationship the therapist had formed with her client, mentally noting how open, kind and yet firm she was with the older man.

Mary finally patted his back. "What do you say, Clyde? Are you willing to give Ava a try for your next visit?"

Ava smiled. "I'd be happy to work with you next week, Mr. Watkins."

The gentleman peered at her, then softened his expression and shrugged. "I suppose I'd be willing to give her a try." He turned to Ava. "But I'm not going to be called Mr. Watkins. That was my dad. You'll have to call me Clyde."

Mary helped him out of his seat, then nodded at his wife. "All right then. Tell Katie to set you up with Ava. It was good to see you again."

When they'd exited, she shut the door and turned toward Ava. "You, my dear, have just received the biggest compliment of any therapist who's graced our office."

She frowned, trying to remember everything Clyde Watkins had said to her. She knew he'd been sizing her up during the session. Though he'd followed through with the exercises Mary guided, Ava could tell he'd paid attention to what she was doing.

Mary pushed the intercom button to her husband's office. "Rick, are you in there?"

His voice carried through the intercom. "Yeah. I've got a client in five minutes."

Mary pushed the button again. "Can you come here a sec?"

"Sure." Within a few moments, he walked into the room. "Is something wrong?"

Mary smiled toward Ava, who swallowed the knot in her throat. Her boss seemed pleased, but Ava had no idea what she had done. Mary pointed toward her. "Ava will be leading Clyde Watkins's therapy session next time."

Rick's eyebrows rose. "No way."

His wife nodded. "Can you believe that?"

Rick smiled as he patted Ava on the back. "Your sweet, humble spirit shines through. Mary and I both knew you were the right addition to our clinic that very first interview."

Ava's heart swelled at the sincere praise of her bosses, and she'd done nothing to deserve it. She understood fully why the Millers had more clients than they had time in a day. Their encouragement was heartwarming. "But I didn't do—"

Mary placed her hand on Ava's. "We know you're a good therapist. You have the education, the recommendations, the references that tell us you know your job. But not everyone has the right heart."

Rick added, "Clyde won't go to anyone but Mary. The old coot won't even see me."

Mary gently elbowed him in the gut. "You're just jealous." She turned to Ava. "Seriously, we've had interns come and go. Clyde has always said no to their assistance." She looked at her husband. "We've always joked that if we found someone Clyde approved of, we'd keep him or her forever."

Rick lifted his arms in surrender. "Guess that means you can stay, but I'm going to have to find other work. The man still won't see me."

Mary giggled as she placed a quick kiss on his cheek. Ava drank in the affection between the two. She'd rarely seen a couple with such open, sincere appreciation for each other. It was what she longed for in a relationship.

An image of Holden developed in her mind. She shook her head, reminding herself she was at her place of business.

"I feel very honored." As Ava spoke the words, thankfulness to God for leading her to this job washed over her afresh.

Mary looked at her. "Do God's guiding with a humble spirit, and you'll never go wrong."

Holden pushed away from the kitchen table. "Dad, I don't think I've eaten this much for breakfast…" he thought for a moment, calculating how many years it had been since the younger of his two sisters married "…in more than three years."

His dad stood, scooping up their plates, and turned toward the sink. "I felt like I was wasting away with that stomach bug for more than a week. I was starving." He put the lid on the butter. "You do dishes."

"No problem." Holden made his way to the sink and turned on the hot water.

His father stuffed the jelly, milk and butter in the refrigerator, then turned back to Holden, leaning against the counter. "Listen, I was thinking about riding into town today." He nodded toward the table. "Read in the paper that the electronics store has those Blu-ray disc players on sale…."

Holden bit back a chuckle as he nodded. Ever since his sister Traci had bought him a DVD player for Christmas, their dad had become a complete movie junkie. But Holden had to admit he hadn't helped matters much when he'd purchased surround sound for him two weeks later. "Don't worry, Dad. I'll take care of the ranch. You just head on into town."

"No, no." His dad shook his head. "I'm going to help you get the work done that needs doing. I just wondered if you'd go with me." He picked up a towel and started drying the dishes Holden had washed.

Holden couldn't get his dad to invest in a dishwasher. He always said that two measly men didn't need a dishwasher. Didn't cook enough to need one. Holden took in the various pans that had contained scrambled eggs, hash browns, bacon and biscuits. Today, two measly men could have used one.

His dad's voice interrupted his thoughts. "You know I don't know enough about that newfangled electronic stuff. I don't want to get ripped off."

"Sure. I'll go with you." Holden hurried through the rest of the dishes, and minutes later they headed to the barn. Work moved quickly with his dad back on his feet after battling pneumonia and pleurisy over the winter, then a stomach bug a week ago. Before lunchtime the two were driving on the Sun Valley Parkway toward Surprise.

Holden sneaked a peek at his dad in the passenger seat of his truck. He noticed, as he had so many times over the last few months, that his father had started looking older than his sixty-two years. Deep wrinkles traced his forehead, the sides of his eyes and along his mouth. But it wasn't the wrinkles that worried Holden; it was the deep, dark circles beneath his dad's eyes. Seeing Ava's aunt Irene looking young and spry at her surprise party also confirmed that his dad seemed to be aging quicker than Holden would have thought.

He pulled into the parking lot of the electronics store, and almost before he could take the keys from the ignition, his dad was making his way into the building. The warm spring sun wrapped Holden as he stepped out of the air-conditioned truck. Arizona was too hot and dry for some people, but he relished the heat against his skin.

The store's cool air blasted him as he walked inside. He glanced toward the DVD players, but didn't spy his dad. He was heading to that aisle anyway when he heard a familiar voice. "Get on over here, Holden."

He turned and saw Irene motioning to him. Ava stood to her right, her head lowered and her hands shoved in her blue jeans pockets. He swallowed. There was something about a gal in blue jeans, especially Ava. The denim practically screamed for him to loop his fingers around her waist and lift her closer to him.

"You heard the woman." Holden's dad stood beside Ava's aunt who held several CDs. "Irene's going to sing in Senior Idol. She wants some help picking out a song."

Holden furrowed his brows as he walked toward them. The smell of Ava's perfume sent his mind into a spin, but he was determined to focus. "Senior Idol?"

"Sure. It's a knockoff of American Idol. You have to be fifty or older. You can sing, dance, whatever talent you want to showcase." Irene picked up another CD. "It's at Willow Canyon High School in July. I know it's only March, but I need to start practicing."

"So, you're picking out a song?"

"What does it look like she's doing, son? Buying dough-nuts?" His dad clicked his tongue.

Holden glanced at Ava. She was staring intently at a CD, one that contained only male song choices. He picked it up and leaned closer to her, whispering in her ear, "Is there one on here you think she should try?"

He heard Ava's slight gasp as she shook her head. His nearness still affected her. He knew it did. It had to, because at any moment he was going to lose control and play caveman, picking her up and carrying her out to his truck. The idea proved too enticing, and he forced himself to step away from her.

"Aunt Irene, you sing anything beautifully. Just pick a song." Holden noted that Ava's voice quivered as she spoke.

"We've only been here an hour. Just hold your—"

"This one." Holden's dad's voice interrupted as he shoved a CD into Irene's hand.

"Bette Midler's 'The Rose'?"

Irene closed her eyes and began to sway slowly as a song Holden hadn't heard since he was a young boy spilled from her lips. He looked at Ava, whose face reddened as her aunt's voice grew in volume. Irene did sing beautifully, but Holden knew Ava hated to be the center of attention.

The words of the song struck Holden as he stared at his woman. *Love, a hunger, an aching need?* Yes, he knew that ache, that desperate need. How many times since Ava ran had he wanted her to come back to Surprise? He'd planned to marry her. Share the burdens of the ranch. Share his concern for his dad. Share his faith, his home, his children. Young or not, he'd wanted her.

Holden grabbed her arm and pulled her several steps away from her aunt and his father. Startled, she looked up, and he peered into her eyes. "We have to talk."

"Yes, we do."

"I'm going to come get you and take you to dinner. Tonight."

Holden expected her to argue, to make up an excuse to stay away from him, but he was determined. He would talk to her tonight even if he had to spend the night sitting outside her aunt's house until Ava opened the door.

To his surprise, she nodded. "All right."

A bump to his shoulder shifted his attention to a tall brunette with freckles splattering her nose and cheeks. She batted her eyes. "Holden Whitaker, seems like months since I've laid eyes on you."

"Hey, Jess, I'm pretty sure it's only been a few weeks."

Jessica Thomas laced her arm around his elbow. "Haven't seen you with Jakey, either. The two of you have a fight?"

She knew good and well what had happened between him and Jake. Holden had never wanted to take his best friend's little sister on a date, but the two of them had hounded him until he'd finally agreed. When Holden didn't promise to waltz her down the aisle after a couple of challenging dates, Jake had gotten mad. Exactly what Holden expected to happen, which was why he hadn't wanted to take her out to begin with. Twenty-three or not, she was still like a little sister to him.

"I'm sorry. I must have missed your friend." Jess released his arm and extended her hand to Ava. "I'm Jessica Thomas, a *good* friend of Holden's, and you are?"

Ava reached for her hand, but Jess pulled back and cocked her head. "Wait a minute. I know you." She snapped her fingers. Her face blanched. "You're that…"

"Ava Herbert." Ava took Jess's hand and shook it. "You might not remember me. It's been a few years since Holden and I dated."

Ava's cheeks bloomed bright pink. Holden chewed the inside of his cheeks, trying not to laugh aloud at her expression. He could still read her thoughts, and right now, she was realizing how much she sounded like a jealous teenager. He didn't mind. Even kind of liked it.

Holden clapped Jess's back. "Tell Jake I'd love to hear from him."

"Sure." All signs of flirtation had left Jess's countenance as she headed down the aisle. "See ya later."

Holden turned back to Ava. "Seven o'clock, okay?"

"You dated Jessica Thomas. Isn't she a little young for you?"

"She's not all that young. Just three years younger than you."

Ava's cheeks flushed again, and she shook her head. "I'm sorry. Of course she's not too young. It's none of my business, anyway."

She tried to step away, but Holden grabbed her wrist. She gazed up at him. Mesmerized by her eyes, yearning to touch her soft cheek, he swallowed. "We're going to dinner. Seven o'clock. All right?"

She lifted her hand to his cheek. Warmth surged through him at the feel of her soft touch. She whispered, "Please forgive me."

"I already have."

Sadness clouded her eyes and her expression fell. She turned away from him. "We'll see."

Chapter 3

Two days had passed since Ava called Holden to cancel their dinner date.

"You're not sick, Ava. You're avoiding me." His voice still rang through her head. *"I'm sorry about what happened. I take all the blame."*

He could say the words, but he couldn't take all the blame. She was every bit as much at fault. She'd been overcome with love and promises and kisses and…she'd made the choice. He hadn't forced anything.

"I think you've met all the regulars." Mary's voice snapped Ava from her thoughts.

"Everyone's been very welcoming," Ava replied.

Her boss slipped a pen beneath the clip of the clipboard. "Not only are you a terrific therapist, but you're Irene Hall's niece."

"I didn't know my aunt knew so many people. I mean, she's active at church, and First Church has a large congregation, but…"

Mary shook her head. "Your aunt is the queen of Senior Idol. You've never seen her perform?"

Ava shook her head.

"That's right. Senior Idol started after you went to college." Mary touched Ava's forearm. "Honey, your aunt has been the crowd favorite. All five years. She never wins, mind you."

Ava frowned. "Why not?"

"Once you win, you can't perform anymore. The seniors' group that puts on the show wants to give everyone a chance."

"I see." She wrinkled her nose. "Sorta."

Mary chuckled. "The city loves her. Have you at least heard her sing?"

"Of course, but—"

"You don't think she's good?"

"Well, yes, she's wonderful. I just didn't know the event was so popular."

"We even get volunteers to bus every able resident from the nursing homes to the high school to watch. We have a blast." She nodded. "You should consider helping out."

"I think I will."

After finishing her charts, Ava said goodbye and drove home. Aunt Irene had left a note on the table saying she'd gone to pick up Mexican, so Ava slipped out of her clothes and into the shower. Her mind wandered to Holden, and whether he'd asked Jessica Thomas out on another date. So far Ava enjoyed everything about Surprise, except she couldn't stop thinking about him.

Turning off the shower, she dried her face and stared into the mirror. *At some point, I've got to tell him the truth.*

She ran a brush through her wet hair, still staring at her reflection. *Maybe I don't have to tell him. It won't do any good. I know Holden. It will only hurt him.*

I know Holden. She'd known him only for a summer. Three months after graduating high school. Emotions were high, spiraling out of control. People just didn't find their one true love at eighteen. The idea was preposterous. And she'd been headed to college.

Now, Will Reynolds, her boyfriend during her junior year of college, he'd been a guy she could have fallen in love with. Twenty-one wasn't too young. He'd been kind, considerate, a Christian and a pharmaceutical major. They'd been compatible in all the right ways, and he seemed to like her a lot.

But she hadn't lain awake at night thinking about him. Hadn't imagined what their children would look like, or what it would be like to wake up each morning with him beside her, as she had imagined with Holden.

She slammed the brush onto the sink. "Just stop it."

"You okay in there?" Her aunt's voice sounded from the kitchen.

Ava snarled at the mirror. "I'm okay, Aunt Irene."

"I thought I heard something."

"I'm fine. Just getting dressed."

"Okay. Well, hurry up. Mitch and I are ready to eat."

Ava slipped on a pair of shorts and a T-shirt. *Great, an evening filled with hardware store drama.* She released a breath and closed her eyes. Her thoughts weren't fair. It wasn't Mitch's fault that she couldn't stop thinking about Holden. Besides, her cousin enjoyed having dinner with her and his mom, and he always helped them with anything that needed to be done around the house.

She walked into the dining area and sat down across from Mitch. They joined hands, and he prayed over their food. When she lifted her head, Mitch reached into his front pocket and pulled out a folded piece of paper. "Holden stopped by the shop today to pick up some supplies. Told me to give you this."

Ava opened the note and read, "Stop avoiding me." He'd printed his number below.

Mitch scooped a spoonful of rice onto his plate. "I don't know why the guy doesn't just move on. Half the eligible women in Surprise are after him."

"Now, Mitch," Aunt Irene chided.

"It's true," he continued. "Just in the few minutes Holden was in the store there was a woman ogling him like a dog would a bone."

Ava crunched the note. She took back her kind thoughts. Mitch needed to get out of her business and find himself a wife.

Holden folded the top piece of the cardboard box to create the windshield for the boxcar. He cut out the rectangle while four of the boys from his church group scurried around collecting paper plates for wheels, plastic cups for headlights, and paint, brushes and glue. Once he'd finished cutting, he taped the windshield in place. Pointing to the directions, he looked at the oldest boy in the group. "Sean, you understand how to finish?"

"We know how to do it," piped up six-year-old Zack. "My uncle and I have done it before."

"Bet mine and my dad's would be better," retorted his friend John.

"Nuh-uh." Zack shook his head, making his fiery-red curls bounce.

"Now that's enough, you two." Holden stared at both of them, the whole time praying he wouldn't burst into laughter.

"We know how to finish," Sean assured him.

"We're ready for you to cut out the windshield, Holden," Vince called from the other side of the room.

"Us, too," said Ben.

"Why don't I help this group, and you help the other?"

Holden turned at the sound of his best friend's voice. "Thanks, Jake."

Jake dipped his chin. "No problem. I've missed these guys the last few weeks."

"I'd say they've missed you as well, right, guys?"

"Yep." Eight-year-old Vince wrapped his arms around Jake's waist.

Holden had a soft spot for Vince. His dad had left before he was born, so it was just Vince and his mom. She was young and nice, tried with everything in her to provide all her son needed. She did a good job, and there were times when Holden wondered if God wanted him to step in, maybe ask Megan out. The little guy needed a dad, and Holden really liked him. A lot.

Once he and Jake had finished making windshields with box cutters, he stood beside his friend and watched as the boys created their team cars.

"Sorry I've been avoiding ya," said Jake.

"It's all right."

"No, it ain't," Jake retorted. "Jess got her head all wrapped around the idea of you and her together. She like to drove us all nuts. You know how she is when she wants something."

Oh, Holden knew. He had many memories of playing at Jake's house as kids. Anytime his little sister wanted to play, or wanted their toys, she'd pitch a fit until the whole family decided she could have whatever it was she wanted. Most stubborn little thing he'd ever known. Which was why he'd never wanted to go out with her in the first place.

"I think she's decided to shift her sights onto Nate Yocum."

Poor guy. Nate was a great man, but he wouldn't have the backbone to turn Jess away if she truly decided she wanted him. If Jake wouldn't punch him in the gut, Holden would bet his friend that the two would be married in a year.

"She said she saw you at the electronics store. And that Ava was there. Is that right?"

Holden nodded. Zack and John started to fight over a paintbrush. Holden snapped his fingers, and Sean handed John a different brush.

"I heard she's working with the Millers."

Holden nodded once more. "She is."

"You two talking again?"

He wished. Today he'd sent a note with Mitch, asking her to give him a call. For months the guilt over what they'd done, and the fact that she wouldn't speak to him, had sickened him. He'd asked God's forgiveness, even fessed up with the truth to his dad. Holden had never meant to hurt her.

No one else knew. Not even Jake. Only Holden's father, and he'd shown Holden in scripture how God had already forgiven him. But he'd wanted to tell Ava, to assure her of his love, to set a date for them to become husband and wife.

But she'd run, and refused to talk to him or see him again.

If only he could undo that night, that moment of weakness. Ugh. Seeing her, knowing she was so close, brought back the battle that had waged within him. He never wanted to forget that night, and yet he wished he could take it back.

Holden looked at Jake and shook his head. "Not really."

"But you'd like to?"

He shrugged. What good would lying do?

"I guess it's true you never get over your first love," Jake said.

Holden chuckled. "So, you still got a thing for Becca Fields from ninth grade? I think her husband and two kids might have something to say about that."

Jake huffed. "I fell in love long before ninth grade."

Holden bit the inside of his lip, trying to remember all the girls Jake had swooned over. For such an overgrown country guy, he'd fallen in love with one girl after another during their school years. Holden snapped his fingers. "Annie Jake. Sixth grade. You loved her last name."

Jake chortled as he pounded his chest with his fist. "My true love goes further back than middle school."

Holden crossed his arms. "You've got to be messing with me."

Jake shrugged.

The door opened and Megan stepped inside. She still wore her uniform, and Holden knew she'd put in a long day at the nursing home. Jake's expression fell and he stood up straighter. "How's it going, Megan?"

"Great." She tucked a strand of dark hair behind her ear. Vince rushed to her and wrapped his arms around her waist. She kissed the top of his head. "Thanks so much. Vince loves this class."

Jake stepped toward them and patted Vince on the shoulder. "He's a great kid." He tousled the boy's hair. "Be good for your mom now."

"I will." Vince offered Jake another hug, and Holden noted the flush that spread up his best friend's neck and onto his cheeks.

Once Megan and Vince left, Holden nudged Jake's arm. "I think I remember. It was kindergarten."

He pursed his lips.

Holden continued, "And her name was Megan Fallows."

Jake pressed his index finger against his mouth. "Hush, man. The boys will hear you."

Holden laughed. "You need to ask her out."

Jake shrugged again.

"Seriously. You'd be great together."

"You think so?"

"I do." Holden punched his arm.

Jake rubbed the spot. "What was that for?"

"We sound like a pair of women."

His friend laughed. "I think you're right."

They leaned against the wall and crossed their arms while the boys continued to work on their cars. Holden glanced at Jake. "So, you gonna ask her?"

Jake smacked his hands against his legs. "Fine. I'll ask her."

Chapter 4

*T*ucked securely under her cowboy's arm, Ava drank in the ever-shrinking yellow sphere as it made its way behind the White Tank Mountains. A pinkish-orange ring circled the sun and faded into a violet-blue August sky. Creosote bushes as well as saguaro and barrel cacti dotted the dry ground. A curve-billed thrasher flew from the top of one of the saguaro toward the sunset, probably to his home, so he could bed down for the night. The thought sent a shiver of fear and excitement down and back up Ava's spine. Holden exhaled a contented breath, and she gazed up into the eyes of the man she loved. He gently cupped her chin with his hand. "I know it sounds corny, Ava—" Holden traced her jaw with his thumb "—but I never want to see another sunset without you."

Ava opened her eyes and gazed at the pale blue ceiling. She'd dreamed about Holden. Again. She rolled to her side and curled her legs around a pillow. Eight years had passed since the young cowboy had made that statement. Eight years of her attending and graduating from college then physical therapy school, working with rehabilitation patients, reestablishing a relationship with God, and… Ava didn't want to think of the *and*. The memory gouged and ripped at her heart, leaving her wounded and scarred in ways she'd never imagined possible. She closed her eyes and sucked in a deep breath. How could a heart feel such pain and yet still beat?

She shifted her head to see the alarm clock. Just past seven, but Ava knew she wouldn't sleep another moment. *So much for sleeping in on my day off.* Slipping out from under the covers, she got dressed, then grabbed a granola bar and a few bottles of water. She scratched out a note for Aunt Irene, then headed toward the mountains.

Walking her favorite dirt-and-rock-covered trail, Ava sucked in a deep breath. She still loved this place. Arizona had been blessed with a rainy winter, and now in March, the regional park was especially beautiful. Cacti reached stoically toward the cloud-dotted blue sky, while yellow brittlebush, red coachwhip, blue dicks, and desert lavender dotted the ground. She plucked a brittlebush flower, examining its bright petals.

She plucked a petal. "He loved me." She plucked another. "He loved me not." She continued until the final petal, which she caressed with her finger. Pulling it free, she whispered, "He loved me."

Twirling the stem, she allowed her gaze to wander across the majesty of the mountains. She looked up at the clouds. "God, I believe he did love me."

With a sigh, she tossed the stem to the ground. In a matter of weeks, the temperatures would rise and the rains would cease, and much of the colorful foliage would die. "They can only last a season," Ava muttered to herself.

But they return when the time is right.

A slow smile curled her lips at the thought. She'd left her beloved Holden Whitaker, as well as Surprise, Arizona, eight years ago. She'd believed she'd be gone forever, that in time the memories would dissipate. But she was back. Given how much she enjoyed her new position at Miller Physical Therapy Clinic, she might be here for good. And Holden wanted to get back together. She saw the forgiveness in his eyes.

She glanced at the fallen petals and stem beside her feet. Summer would return to Surprise, but this flower wouldn't. It had been plucked from its base and would never bloom again. She swallowed back the truth of the analogy that had drifted into her mind. Returning to Surprise to live didn't mean she could have Holden's heart again. One day soon she would tell him the truth.

And she knew he'd never forgive her.

Holden guided the ten boys from his church group along the trail. Once a month he took any who could attend on some kind of field trip. March proved to be a great time to take them to the White Tans Mountains to hike, eat a picnic lunch and play games.

"You don't think we'll see any snakes, do you, Holden?" asked six-year-old John.

Holden glanced down and saw the boy's eyes were nearly as large as the soccer balls they'd brought with them.

"Duh, we'll see snakes," Zack chided. "We're outside. In the mountains."

John reached over and grabbed Holden's fingers. "We will?"

Holden squeezed the boy's hand. "We might, but we'll be careful. No snake's going to ruin our fun."

"Phew." Zack jumped up and down with his fists raised, his red curls bouncing around his face. "If a snake comes up to us, I'll punch it right in the nose."

Holden patted his shoulder. "All right, Muhammed Ali. Let's keep walking."

Zack pulled away. "My name ain't Mountain Owie. I'm Zack."

Jake walked up beside him and flicked one of the boy's curls. "You're right about that, little buddy."

Holden noticed a woman a ways down the trail, sitting on the edge of a large rock. Poor lady. Her quiet morning was about to be invaded by ten active boys and two men. She must have heard them because she turned around, and Holden's heartbeat raced. *Ava.*

Jake nudged his arm. "I'll take the boys on ahead. You be a man and stop and talk to her."

Holden grinned at his friend. "You talk to Megan yet, Mr. Macho Man?"

Jake spread his arms. "You see Megan around here?"

Holden pointed at him. "Your day is coming, my friend."

"Yeah, but your day is here." Jake chortled as he turned his attention to Ava, then extended his hand once they'd gotten close enough. "Hello, Ava. Remember me?"

She stood and took his hand. "Hello, Jake."

Zack cocked his head and squinted up at her. "Who's the lady?"

"She's Holden's friend, Ava." Jake snapped his fingers. "Come on, guys. Let's keep walking while he talks to her for a minute."

"Is she his girlfriend?" asked Vince.

Zack shook his hips, then made kissing noises. "She's his girlfriend."

Holden nudged the boy forward. The little redhead

seemed determined to drive him crazy at every angle possible. "You need to stay with Jake."

He waited until the boys were several yards away before he turned to Ava. She looked great with her hair pulled back in a short ponytail and her face free of makeup. Like the girl he'd fallen in love with.

"That's quite a bunch of boys you've got there." She brushed a strand of hair away from her cheek.

"Some of my boys' group from church."

She furrowed her brows. "You lead a children's group?"

He nodded. "Just boys. First through sixth grade, on Wednesday nights." He pointed toward them. "Jake helps out a lot, especially on our monthly outings."

Ava clasped her hands together. "That's great, Holden. Really good of you."

"I don't do it to be good. I love kids. Teaching them is one way I can serve God."

"I know. I remember how much you loved children."

She looked away from him, and Holden fought the urge to cup her chin and force her gaze up to his. "You didn't call me."

"Well, I…"

He reached for her arm, then stopped and shoved his hand in his front pocket. "I'm sorry, Ava. I didn't mean to hurt you. If I'd known you'd run like that, I would have—"

She shook her head. "I don't blame you. I was never mad at you."

"But you wouldn't talk to me. I tried your parents, your aunt, even went to the college."

"I know." She looked up at him. "I'm sorry, Holden. Truly. If I could go back and do things differently, I would."

Holden couldn't stop himself. He took her hand. "We can start over, Ava. The past is done. I'd really like to try."

"So much happened after I left, Holden. Things you don't know about it." She gazed past him and bit her bottom lip. "Things I should tell you…"

"What? You dated other people?" Holden laughed. "Ava, I don't care about that." He lifted one eyebrow. "I might have had a date or two myself since you left."

She looked back at him, and a slow smile curved her lips. "Would Jessica Thomas possibly have been one of them?"

Holden blew out a breath. "Ugh. That girl was merciless as a kid, and she's just as bad as a woman."

Ava giggled.

"Please. Let me take you on a date. I'll pick you up tonight. Seven o'clock."

Ava stared at him for what felt like an eternity before she finally nodded. "Okay."

Holden kissed her forehead. "I better get back to Jake. He's got his hands full with Zack all by himself. Add nine more boys and…"

"Zack's the redhead, right?"

"How'd you guess?"

"That one's a little firecracker."

Holden chuckled. "That's putting it lightly. More like a terror. If my sisters have their wish, I'll have two or three just like him."

Ava's expression changed, and she looked away. "About tonight…"

"I'll pick you up at seven." Before she could back out, Holden hustled down the trail after his friend and the boys. He had no idea what he'd said to switch her mood so quickly, and he had no intention of dwelling on it.

He bit back a chuckle as he caught up with the guys. She was worried he'd be mad she'd gone on a few dates in the last eight years. Dates didn't bother him. She was still single, and so was he. And he couldn't wait to get to know her again. She was the only girl he'd ever considered making him a married man. And he couldn't deny that she still was.

Chapter 5

Holden buckled the thin brown belt, then lifted his shoulders to survey himself in the mirror. He'd pressed his navy blue and white striped polo shirt and khaki pants. Rarely wore the dress clothes. Didn't even wear them to church, but he figured he'd cleaned up pretty well for his date with Ava. She liked to doll up, and she'd appreciate if he took a little extra time on himself.

After slipping on his loafers, he walked into the kitchen to grab his keys off the rack. Dad whistled, and Holden's cheeks warmed, knowing an interrogation would ensue.

"Don't you look all spiffy," his father commented.

Holden nodded as he shoved his wallet into his back pocket.

"Got a hot date or something? Can't remember the last time I saw you so dressed up."

"Yep."

"Who's the lucky girl? You must like this one." His dad clicked his tongue and furrowed his eyebrows.

The his phone rang, and Holden exhaled a sigh of relief that he didn't have to answer. He waved and mouthed a goodbye, but his dad lifted a finger for him to wait. "Two of 'em? Is the fence down somewhere?"

Holden's stomach tightened.

"The gate was open!" Dad scratched his jaw, then raked his fingers through his graying hair. "Coulda sworn I locked it."

Holden walked back to his bedroom and changed into his jeans and an older work shirt. He texted Ava to let her know he wouldn't be able to make it for their date, and that he'd call her later. *I finally get her to agree to go out, and I'm the one who has to cancel.*

His dad said goodbye, then hollered down the hall. "Two of the cows got out. They're in the road, not wanting to budge."

"What I figured from hearing your side of the conversation." Holden clamped his lips together, willing himself not to fuss at him for leaving the gate unlocked. Again.

"Daryl's trying to keep 'em from getting hit, but we've gotta help corral them back behind the fence."

"I know, Dad." Holden's tone was sharp, and he chewed the inside of his cheek to keep from saying anything more.

"I'm sorry, son. You'll need to get hold of your girl."

"I texted her."

"I'll get the truck. You get some corn feed and the Wiffle bat. Might get a Hot-Shot, too, just in case. Daryl said it's Betty and her calf. You know she's gonna be difficult."

Holden didn't respond as he started toward the barn to get the electric cattle prod. With each step, his frustration mounted, until he finally grabbed the prod and closed his eyes for a quick prayer. *God, I know Dad didn't mean to ruin my date. If she agreed to go once, she'll agree again. Temper my frustration.*

He exhaled a long breath before walking to the truck. The past year had been physically hard on his dad. Lately, he'd been forgetting or halfway doing things. The behaviors were in complete contrast to the man who'd raised Holden. His dad needed to slow down. His body couldn't do the work he'd done forty years ago. But how could Holden tell him the time had come to give up some of the work? He loved the ranch, loved to work hard. He'd spent his life raising cattle.

Within moments they reached the gate on the west side of the ranch. His brother-in-law Daryl had been right. It was Betty, and she was none too happy to move from her spot in the road.

"Let's try to get her calf first," said Dad. "Maybe if the baby moves Betty will follow."

Daryl nodded. "I'll watch for traffic."

"Sounds like a plan." Holden held out a palmful of corn feed in front of Betty's calf. "Come on, girl. Let's get out of the road."

"Come on now, girl." Dad touched the calf's leg to prod her to move. Betty mooed, and Dad shifted away from the fifteen-hundred-pound animal.

The calf took a few steps toward Holden, stretching out her neck to sample the feed. He allowed her a few nibbles, then walked farther back off the road. "Good job, girl. Keep on coming."

The calf continued to move, but Betty mooed again and blew out a huff. Stubborn old girl was mad at Dad. The calf continued to walk toward Holden as he gave her bites of feed. "Dad, you and Daryl switch spots. Betty's mad at you."

Dad bristled. "She's always mad at me. Cantankerous old woman."

Daryl piped up. "I think Holden's right. Hand me the Wiffle bat."

With a grunt, Dad switched spots, and Holden again realized how his father needed a break from the pressures on the ranch. Holden guided the calf back through the gate, and with a few prods of the bat and encouraging words, they were able to get Betty safely back inside the fence. He checked, then pulled on the gate to be sure it locked.

Dad shook hands with Daryl. "Thanks for letting me know, son."

"No problem. I'm just glad no one hit them."

"Me, too." Holden shuddered at the thought of someone getting killed hitting one of their cows. Betty was worth a good chunk of money, but the thought of someone losing his or her life was much worse.

He needed to talk with Dad. Holden and Daryl could take over the ranch. Dad could still do some of the work, just not so much. Noting the aggravation etched on his brow, however, Holden knew today wouldn't be a good time for that talk.

Once back at the house, he washed up, then tried to call Ava. Just as he feared, her phone went straight to voice mail. Part of him wanted to hop in the truck and head over to Irene's house. See if Ava would at least go with him for a cup of coffee. But he decided against it. He didn't want their first date to be half done. He wanted to be able to treat her like a queen, show her just how much he'd missed her. So he'd wait. Maybe she'd call him tomorrow.

Ava pulled the chart out of the tray and looked at the name: Clyde Watkins. It was her first day completely solo and her last patient before lunch. *I hope he likes me as much this week as he did last week.*

Plastering a smile on her lips, she opened the door to

the private room and spotted a grimacing old man. She placed the chart on the small counter. "How are we doing today, Clyde?"

"Clyde, huh?" he grumbled. "All you young folks today. No show of respect."

She crossed her arms in front of her chest. "I'm fine with addressing you as Mr. Watkins. Last week you told me to call you Clyde."

"Humph." He pursed his lips, then pressed his fists against his hips. "Arthritis is killing me today. Might want to get Mary in here."

"She is with another patient. Have you taken your prescribed medicine today?"

"Of course," he snapped. "You think I won't take medicine to make me feel better?"

Ava flipped a page on his chart. "Well, Mary noted that you're not fond of how the medicine makes you tired, and that sometimes you try to skip it."

Clyde narrowed his eyes. "She wrote that, huh?"

Ava nodded and kept her gaze locked with his.

He smacked his hands together. "Okay. Fine. I haven't taken the medicine yet. Let's just do the exercises, so I can go home, take the pill, then get a nap."

Ava chewed her lip to keep from grinning. "Sounds like a plan to me. Let's start with the seated hip march. You ready? Sit up straight."

"I know how to sit." Clyde sat up and kicked back his left foot, keeping his toes on the floor.

"Great. Now lift your right foot. Two. Three. Four. Five. Lower your foot. Now, lift again."

Clyde continued to complain throughout the session, but Ava stayed firm, focused and kind. Once finished, on impulse she offered him a quick hug. "You did a great job. Now go home and rest."

Clyde's lip curved up slightly on the left. "I suppose you did all right, as well. I'll see you next week."

Ava recorded the visit in the computer, then looked up when Katie stopped beside her. She grinned at the perplexed expression on the college girl's face then shrugged. "What?"

"Clyde Watkins scheduled his next appointment with you."

Ava chuckled. "I know. Crazy, huh?"

"Crazier than you know." Katie shifted her weight from one foot to the other. "Are you free for lunch?"

"Sure. I was going to pick up some fast food."

"There's a sub place down the block. We could walk."

Ava grabbed her purse and followed her young friend. Katie was quiet as they walked. Her shoulders slumped and her chin dipped, and Ava knew she wanted advice. Ava lifted a quick prayer to God. She hadn't made the best choices at Katie's age, and she wasn't sure what the girl was about to divulge.

After ordering their lunches, they slipped into a booth. Katie reached for her sandwich, and Ava said, "Let's say a quick prayer first."

Katie nodded and put down the food. They bowed their heads as Ava led them in prayer. Inwardly, she asked the Holy Spirit to guide their lunch and anything she said to Katie.

Katie took a bite of her sandwich, then swallowed a gulp of her soft drink. She wiped her mouth, then looked at Ava. "I'm in love with a guy."

Ava chewed her food. She hadn't been in Surprise long, though she'd had a few interviews with the Millers before accepting the position. She hadn't heard of Katie having a boyfriend, and neither Mary nor Rick had mentioned it. She patted her mouth. "How long have you been dating?"

"Three months."

Ava coughed. She jerked up her napkin and covered her mouth, then took a sip of her drink. The same amount of time she'd dated Holden.

"You okay?"

Ava nodded as she wiped the corners of her eyes. "Just went down the wrong way."

Katie twirled her own napkin. "He loves me, too." Her cheeks bloomed pink and she ducked her head. "Said he wants to marry me."

"Have your parents met him?"

She shook her head. "No. But they'd love him. He's a Christian. Majoring in law enforcement. He's a really great guy."

Ava shifted in her seat. She took a bite of a baked chip, then another swallow of her drink. "Okay. So, let them meet him."

"It's not that simple." Katie propped both elbows on the table. "I didn't do well on my anatomy test. Got a D. That means the best I can do in the class is a C, and that's only if I get an A on the final."

Ava furrowed her brows. "I'm not sure what this has to do with your boyfriend."

"Well, he graduates in May, and he's trying to get a job in Phoenix. He wants to get married and move there." Katie stared down at her sandwich. "And maybe I'm not cut out for college." She dropped her hands on the table. "I mean, I hate it."

Ava racked her mind for the right words to say. She wanted to tell her not to drop out of school, to wait to get married. And yet part of her wished she had married Holden and waited for college. The world would recommend school, then marriage, for stability, but was that always God's will for everyone? *God, show me what to say.*

She looked across the table. Katie was staring at her, her expression pleading for understanding and wisdom. *She's reaching out for help, God, and she's asking probably the worst person in the world for advice.*

Ava's mind cleared, and relief washed over her as she knew exactly what to say to the young woman. She reached across the table and placed her hand on Katie's. "I can't tell you whether you should get married, stay in school, both or neither. I can tell you not to run. Don't run from your parents, from your boyfriend or from your school. Introduce him to Rick and Mary. Sit down together. Have an honest, open conversation, and ask God to guide you all."

Katie blew out a breath, then took another sip of her drink. "I think you're right." She dropped her shoulders. "In fact, I feel better already."

As Katie chattered about her boyfriend and her hopes for the future, Ava nibbled her lunch and listened. At the same time, her mind churned over the advice she'd given. She couldn't run anymore, either. She needed to tell Holden everything. The sooner the better, or she might lose courage again.

Chapter 6

Holden picked up a stick of deodorant and a bottle of shampoo, then got in line with his dad at the pharmacy. The doctor hadn't been pleased with Dad's blood pressure, the problem Holden had insisted he seek medical help for to begin with. The doc had upped Dad's dose again, and said if he didn't start eating better, he'd wind up having a stroke.

"I knew you weren't telling me the full truth about your blood pressure," Holden whispered.

"What's there to tell? Nothing I can do about it."

Holden gripped the shampoo so tight he worried the lid might pop and liquid would spew everywhere. Sometimes he just wanted to wring the stubborn man's neck. "We can start eating better. Healthier."

Dad swatted the air. "We eat fine now."

"Obviously, we don't. Your blood pressure was sky-high, and we're in line to have your medication upped. Again."

"What's that you say?"

The Whitaker men turned. Holden spied Irene and Phoebe standing behind them in line. His dad glared at him before he smiled at the women. "Wasn't saying much of anything. How are you ladies doing? Irene, haven't seen you in quite a while."

"Not since you decided to switch to the early service. Course, I know that's probably better for the ranching."

Holden glanced from his dad to Ava's aunt. Both of them shifted their weight and averted their gazes from each other. If he didn't know better, he'd think they were two teenagers talking to each other for the first time.

Irene continued, "But what was that I heard about blood pressure?"

Dad grimaced. "Ah, it's nothing."

"Jerry Whitaker, don't you lie to me."

Holden blinked and cocked his head. Now, he was positively sure the two were flirting.

Dad lifted his hand and pinched his finger and thumb together. "Just a little high."

"You don't want to mess with that, Jerry," added Phoebe. "My dad didn't pay the doctor any attention. Ended up having a stroke and dying." She snapped her fingers. "Just like that."

Holden looped his fingers around his belt. Well, that sure made him feel better.

"Why don't the two of you come over to my house? I've got some terrific low sodium recipes I can share with you," said Irene.

"Nah, we wouldn't want to impose," said Dad.

Holden furrowed his brows. What kind of response was that? Dad had practically asked Irene to insist.

"No. I insist."

Just as Holden figured.

"I'll cut up some fruit. Brew some tea." She rubbed her

hands together. "And I've been practicing my song. You could be my first audience."

Dad's face lit up like a sunrise on a hot July day. "Well, if you don't mind…"

Phoebe rested her palm against her stomach. "I think I'll have you drop me off at my house before you go home, if that's all right."

Irene patted her friend's arm. "Of course." She leaned toward Dad. "She's getting medicine for her bowels. Been having a lot of trouble lately."

Holden rolled his eyes. He had to get out of this place. Between the flirting and the bodily function honesty, he felt as though he might be getting sick.

He glanced at his phone to check the time. Too early for Ava to get off work. He inwardly growled, knowing he had plenty of work to do at the ranch. He looked at his dad and Irene making goo-goo eyes at each other. But when had this happened?

Jake and Megan. Now Dad and Irene. Everyone seemed to be falling for someone, but Holden couldn't seem to work things out with the woman he wanted.

Once at Irene's house, he settled into a red leather recliner and looked through the pile of cookbooks she insisted they take home. He tried not to listen to his dad's and Irene's occasional giggles and muffled conversation as they cut up fruit and made tea in the kitchen.

They were close enough in age. Probably even went to school together, since they both grew up in Surprise. And he couldn't deny his dad might enjoy some company as he got older. Soon Holden's sisters would be having grandbabies, and if he had his way, he'd settle down, as well. Plus, Irene was one of the best women he knew. Still, the thought of his dad and a woman, in love… Holden shivered. It just seemed…well, gross.

"Here ya go, Holden." Irene handed him a bowl of mixed fruit and a glass of iced tea.

"Thanks."

She pointed to the cookbooks. "Did you see any good recipes in there?"

"Well, I…"

She clapped, then turned toward Dad, who'd taken a seat across from Holden and had just shoveled a bit of fruit into his mouth. "I've got an idea."

"What's that?" asked Dad.

"I want the two of you to come over for dinner tomorrow night. I'll make grilled salmon and…" She pressed her finger against her lips. "The rest will be a surprise. What do you say?"

She glanced from Dad to Holden and then back again. By his expression, Holden knew his father would agree to the invitation. And Holden would enjoy eating food that wasn't cooked by him or his dad. But Ava. She might not be as pleased to have the company.

He shook the thought away. She'd agreed to have dinner with him two nights ago. He was the one who'd canceled. Sure, she didn't answer his text, nor did she phone him back when he'd tried to call later, but maybe she'd just been busy. She did have a brand-new job. Plenty of adjustments to make.

"We'd love to come," said Dad. "What would you like us to bring? Holden makes a mean brownie."

Irene placed her hands on her hips. "I thought we were looking into getting your blood pressure lowered."

His dad frowned. "Brownies will raise my blood pressure?"

"Okay. You can have just a little." She giggled, and Holden had to bite back the urge to gag.

He swallowed a gulp of tea. Irene made the best tea

in the Southwest. He placed the glass on a coaster on the table. "I thought you were going to sing for us."

Irene nodded. "I sure said I would. Be right back."

Dad watched her scurry into the next room, his face glowing like a boy with a new bike. Holden took another swig of the tea. Next time he'd let Irene take his father to the doctor. Holden had a feeling Dad would do whatever she said.

Ava took a small bite of brown rice as she watched her aunt's guests. She'd been surprised when Aunt Irene announced Jerry and Holden were coming over for dinner. Glancing down at her lavender sundress, Ava felt her cheeks warm. She'd chosen the dress because Holden told her years ago that she looked pretty in purple.

"I'm not a huge salmon fan usually," Jerry said in a booming voice. He shoveled a scoop of fish and zucchini into his mouth, then swallowed. "But this is delicious. And you say it's good for my blood pressure?"

Aunt Irene's chest puffed out at the praise. "Salmon is good for you anyway, Jerry. Filled with protein, omega 3 fatty acids, and vitamin D. What do you think about the zucchini?"

Jerry wrinkled his nose. "Never been a big fan of vegetables." He stabbed a piece of zucchini with his fork and popped it in his mouth. "But I gotta admit this is good. Plenty of flavor."

"That's the teriyaki." Aunt Irene dabbed the corner of her mouth with her napkin. "Low sodium, of course. You just need to learn to add flavor with spices instead of salt."

Ava sneaked a glance at Holden. He looked handsome, so cleaned up, in a red polo and pressed khaki pants. Not that he wasn't already over-the-top attractive in his usual attire of button-down shirt, blue jeans, cowboy boots and hat. But tonight she couldn't stop herself from drinking in thick dark eyebrows over deep blue eyes. She wanted to run her fingertips across the strong line of his jaw, feel the prickles of his five o'clock shadow. Looking down at her plate, she willed herself to focus on the meal as she cut a piece of salmon with the side of her fork.

"Ava?" said Aunt Irene.

Glancing back up, she realized three pairs of eyes all stared at her. She frowned. "I'm sorry, did you say something?"

Her aunt pointed toward Jerry. "He asked how your new job is going."

Ava smiled, trying to slow the butterflies fluttering in her stomach at Holden's intent gaze. "I love it."

Aunt Irene reached across the table and placed her hand on Jerry's. "Just this week Ava said she believes God brought her back to Surprise for a reason."

Holden's eyebrows rose and a smiled curved his mouth.

"My job," Ava said, clearing her throat. "I feel as though God handpicked it for me."

She focused on finishing her dinner while Jerry and Aunt Irene continued to talk. Many times she felt Holden's gaze on her. Tonight would be a perfect time to confess the whole truth to him, and she prayed God would give her strength.

"I'd love to play a few tunes." Her aunt's voice interrupted Ava's thoughts. "But you have to promise to sing with me."

Jerry guffawed. "Irene, I haven't sung in years."

She waggled her finger. "You can't fool me, Jerry Whitaker. I know you sing. We were in the choir together in high school."

Jerry laughed. "That was years ago."

Ava grinned at the older couple's interaction, and had

to bite back a chuckle at the confused and possibly disgusted expression on Holden's face. Her aunt and his dad had more history than either of them knew about.

Aunt Irene stood and motioned for Jerry to join her. "Come on. I'll play piano, but you gotta sing, too."

Jerry grumbled, but he stood and followed her into the other room. He glanced back at Ava with a quick wink, and she shook her head at his silliness.

"Guess we do dishes."

Her heart flipped at Holden's deep voice, and she stood and stacked the plates onto hers. "I guess so."

Holden gathered several dishes and followed her into the kitchen. He scraped off food and rinsed while she put the leftovers into Tupperware containers. The tune of "Hit the Road, Jack" boomed from the living room. After a few chords Aunt Irene's and Jerry's voices joined the piano.

"I didn't know my dad was in chorus. I've heard him sing on the ranch, but that was usually when he didn't know I was nearby."

"He sounds great." Ava placed the leftovers in the refrigerator. "Maybe you can sing, too, and you just don't know it."

Holden lifted his hands. "No. I'm pretty sure I know I can't sing."

Ava chuckled as she loaded the dishwasher. "Don't Go Breaking My Heart" sounded from the other room. The two sang their parts in perfect time, but the lyrics scratched at the old, unhealed wound in her heart, and she felt Holden's gaze on her again. "You wanna go sit in the backyard?"

"Sure."

As he followed her out the door, she prayed for strength and the right words. *Please God, make him forgive me.*

Though surrounded by houses, she sat in a chair and sucked in the beauty of the purple sky that blended into pink around the bright yellow setting sun. *Just do it. Speak the words. Get it out.* "Holden, I'm sorry I ran."

"No. I'm sorry, Ava. I should have been stronger. I never meant to hurt you."

She peeked at him, noting the regret that etched his face. She wanted to reach out, to take his hand in hers, but if she touched him she'd lose heart. Part of her still loved him. Curling her fingers around the arm of the chair, she shook her head. "It's not only your fault. I lost myself in emotions, as well. We were wrong, and God wanted us to wait until marriage, but I shouldn't have just run away. But we got so serious so fast, and I wasn't ready."

"I wanted to marry you."

"I know." Ava's heart beat faster "And I really wasn't ready for that. I'd only graduated high school a few months before."

Holden pursed his lips. "If I could do it over, I'd have—"

"We can't change what happened, but I should have talked to you. I should have told you about—"

The back door opened and Aunt Irene poked out her head. "You two get in here. I've almost got Jerry talked into doing Senior Idol with me."

Holden's jaw dropped and he stood. "You're kidding. This I gotta hear." He extended his palm to Ava. "You and I are going to have lunch after church tomorrow. Okay?"

Ava battled relief and disappointment that they weren't finishing their conversation. She accepted his hand and cringed at the tingles she still felt at his touch. "Okay."

Chapter 7

Holden stood in the foyer of the church, waiting for second service to end at any moment. He'd spotted Ava's car in the parking lot. He knew she was there, and even though he'd attended first service and Sunday school, he was determined to hang around and wait for her. She might try to wriggle out of lunch, but he had no intention of letting her get away a second time.

The door opened and several people walked out. Jake exited beside Megan, with Vince tagging behind, and Holden smiled. Jake waved, and the three of them walked toward him. "Hey, Holden. Surprised to see you at second service."

"Just waiting on someone." He extended his hand and Vince smacked his palm. "How you doing, man?"

"Jake is taking me and Mom to lunch. We're getting pizza." Vince's eyes lit up. "Then I'm gonna beat Jake at video games."

Holden looked at Jake and Megan. The man beamed with excitement, while she dipped her chin in what appeared to be embarrassed pleasure.

Jake tousled Vince's hair. "Yep. Last time I let him win."

Holden cocked his head. "Last time?"

Vince's face scrunched up. "Nuh-uh. I beat you."

"He's just teasing you." Megan tapped her son's shoulder.

Holden spied Ava. He waved and she moved toward them. "Oh, hi. I didn't see you."

Seeing the bright blush that swallowed her cheeks, Holden wasn't sure if she was fibbing or just nervous. "No problem." He patted his stomach. "I'm getting hungry. Didn't want to miss my lunch date."

Ava opened her mouth, and Holden feared she would try to come up with an excuse to bail. He pointed toward Megan. "Ava, I'm not sure if you've met Megan Fallows. And this is her son, Vince."

Megan nodded, and Vince reached up and held his mom's hand. "Hi." He looked up at Jake, then at Ava. "We're going to have pizza. You and Holden could come with us if you want."

Relief washed across Ava's features as she said, "That sounds like a great idea."

Holden frowned. They wouldn't be able to talk, really talk, with another couple sitting across from them and kids screaming at the arcade games that circled the place.

"Can I go, too? Mom's gotta work today."

Holden turned and saw Zack standing behind him. He tugged at the collar of his polo shirt.

"Zack!" his mom admonished. "You don't invite yourself. Grandma is expecting you to come over. You'll have a good time with her."

Zack crossed his arms in front of his chest. "Grandma makes me eat peanut butter and jelly, then she falls asleep on the couch."

"You like peanut butter and jelly."

"Not as much as pizza."

His mom shook her head. "I'm so sorry. He just says whatever he's thinking."

Holden couldn't help but chuckle at the rambunctious little guy. His private lunch plans with Ava were already ruined. Might as well include Zack, as well.

"Tell you what," Holden said. "Ava and I will take you for pizza, then we'll drop you off at your grandma's house when we're done."

Zack tugged at his mom's shirt. "Can I, Mom? That'll be okay, right?"

"Holden, you don't have to do this."

"It'll be fun," said Ava. She introduced herself to Zack and his mom.

Before Holden had time to comprehend all that had happened, he had Zack buckled into the backseat of his truck, jabbering about some cartoon on television, while they followed Jake, Megan and Vince to the pizza place. After parking, Holden turned to Ava. "This was not the kind of lunch I planned for today."

"What had you planned?"

"I wanted to talk about us."

"Us?" Ava batted her eyes. "What about all the girls you've dated since I left?"

"Jealous?"

She wrinkled her nose. "Nah. Remember, I dated a bunch of guys, too."

Holden fought the urge to bend down and plant a firm kiss on her teasing lips. He liked the flirting, but not the thought of Ava dating other men.

She waved him forward. "Come on. We can talk later. Let's go eat. I'm starving."

The two of them sat at the table with his friends and the kids. The boys ate their pizza in record time, then begged to play games. Holden and Jake gave them money for tokens, and the boys were off. Ava and Megan seemed to get along well, and Holden noted his friend's smitten expression. He envisioned their future as two couples, all friends who got together and hung out with their kids.

With their money spent, the boys returned to the table. Zack plopped onto his chair and took a long swallow of his soft drink. "This place is awesome. I'm gonna tell Mom I wanna have my birthday party here next month."

"Yeah," Vince said. "And I can come, too. Right, Mom?"

Zack pounded the table. "Of course you'll come. And so will John and Ben and Sean…"

Ava touched Zack's wrist as his voice rose with each name he said. "Your birthday is next month? How old will you be?"

He puffed out his chest. "Seven. I'm in second grade."

Ava's face blanched, and she removed her hand and rested it in her lap. Jake, Vince and Zack talked about when and how Zack could have his party. Megan talked to Ava, but her responses were brief, and her countenance had changed.

Holden dropped Zack off at his grandmother's house. Ava didn't talk as he drove back to her car at the church. Maybe she was tired, or the pizza hadn't settled in her stomach well.

When he stopped the truck, she turned to him. He couldn't read her expression. Sadness. Fear. Pain. She bit her bottom lip.

"Ava, I want—"

She shook her head. "No. I can't go out with you. Please, Holden. Too many things have happened."

He reached for her, but she opened the door, jumped into her car, then drove away.

"I did what you said. No running away from my problems for this girl."

Ava looked up as Katie walked toward her. *Wish I could say the same thing about myself.* She forced a smile and leaned against the counter, gripping one of her patient's charts to her chest. "So, you introduced him to your parents?"

Katie's expression brightened. "Yes, and they love him." She wrapped a strand of hair around her finger. "I should have known they would. Corey's perfect."

"I wouldn't go that far." Rick made his way out of their small break area.

Mary followed behind him, rubbing lotion into her hands. "But he is a very nice young man." She wrapped her arm around Ava's shoulder and squeezed. "And I hear we have you to thank for convincing Katie to talk with us."

Katie pulled a tube of ChapStick from her pocket and pressed it against her lips. "I was just scared, you know. Worried y'all wouldn't like Corey. Afraid about what you'd say about my anatomy course."

"Well, we're not thrilled about anatomy," Rick said.

"But we agree," added Mary. "The smartest thing to do is to drop it this semester. You won't be able to get in the nursing program with a C."

"If that's what I decide to do," said Katie.

"Right," said Mary.

Ava looked from Katie to her bosses. "Sounds like you all had a terrific weekend."

"We did," said Mary.

"Even the twins love Corey," said Katie.

"Yep." Rick pointed to the clock. "Getting close to time to open the doors. Let's pray over the week."

He took Ava's hand in his, and Katie held her other one. In their small joined circle, Rick thanked God for the week and asked that they be lights to all the people they encountered. He squeezed Ava's hand as he prayed, "Thank you for bringing Ava to us. She is a terrific addition to our company and a wonderful example to our daughter."

Heat rushed down Ava's chest, making her stomach churn. They didn't know the truth about her. That she'd run from her problems eight years ago and was still running from the truth. She just wanted the memories to go away. If Holden would only leave her alone, she could move forward with her life. *Maybe I shouldn't have come back here.*

Rick and Katie released her hands, then Katie wrapped her in a hug. "I'm so glad you're here."

She hugged Katie back. "Me too." Tightening the embrace for a brief moment, Ava admitted she was glad to be in Surprise, Arizona. She couldn't imagine a better job, and living with Aunt Irene again was pure pleasure every day. Her aunt made Ava feel welcome and needed. She lavished Ava with compliments and challenges, things Ava had never received from her parents.

Rick and Mary left to check some of the equipment, and Ava leaned toward Katie and whispered, "What about the possibility of wedding plans?"

The girl wrinkled her nose. "I didn't tell them about that." She straightened her shoulders. "But that's because Corey and I talked about it after they all met. He really likes them, and he doesn't want to do anything to make them mad at him." She shrugged. "Said we need to start off on the right foot."

"As opposed to the left one."

Katie snapped her fingers. "That's what I said."

Ava laughed. "I'm just kidding. Corey sounds like a smart guy."

"He really is. Besides, he said that Phoenix is only forty minutes away. If he does get a job there, we can still see each other a lot."

"And you can stay in school."

"Yeah." She shoved her hands in her pockets. "And I guess I do want to try. Not sure if I can make it into nursing."

Ava nudged her shoulder as they walked toward the front of the office. "You can make it. No one ever said that things worth having were easy to come by."

Holden's face when she'd jumped out of the truck washed through her mind. Bile rose in her throat, and she swallowed. Placing her palm on her cheek, she forced a smile. "Better take a restroom break while I have the chance."

Katie flopped into her chair. "You better. Clyde is your first client of the day, and he's usually a bit on the grumpy side when he has to come in early."

Ava didn't respond as she made her way to the bathroom. After turning on the cold water, she splashed her face several times, then wiped it with a paper towel. She stared at her pale reflection. *So much for wearing makeup today.*

Her own words to Katie assaulted Ava from every angle. *Don't run. No one ever said that things worth having were easy to come by.* How could she be such a hypocrite? Say all the right things and yet do the opposite?

She turned on the water and splashed her face again. She just needed to stay away from Holden. Change churches if necessary. She enjoyed her aunt's church, but if it meant running into Holden, or being forced to face things that were over and done with, then she'd try somewhere else.

She heard Katie through the door. "Go ahead and have a seat, Clyde. She'll be with you in a minute."

Ava still looked pale. She wet a paper towel and pressed it to her forehead, cheeks and neck one more time. Straightening her shoulders and lifting her chin, she said to her reflection, "You can do this. Focus on the present. Don't dwell on what's past."

Sometimes you have to face the past to move forward with the present.

She shook away the thought as she exited the bathroom. Walking out to the lobby, she waved for Clyde to join her. He frowned. "You don't look like you feel well today."

"Stomach's just a little queasy."

Clyde huffed. "You young folks today. You don't know what queasy is. Why, the doctor put me on some medicine that twists my stomach up into such knots. Ridiculous. You'd think somebody could figure a medicine—"

A wave of nausea washed over Ava. She lifted her finger. "I'm sorry, Clyde. I'll be right back."

"What?" He furrowed his brows. "You really feeling sick or just trying to run away from my appointment?"

Ava raced out of the room and back into the restroom. She dipped her head and leaned her elbows against the sink. Clyde had no idea how true his words were. Not about the appointment. But she was definitely still running.

Chapter 8

Holden shook the fence to be sure the mending stuck. He pointed his hammer at Betty, and she blew out a puff of air. "Not getting out today, old girl." He shook his head at her as he put the hammer in the pouch around his waist. "Haven't ever seen a cow so determined to break out." He opened his arms wide. "It's not like you don't have plenty of places to roam."

Betty mooed, and Holden would have been willing to bet the bovine knew exactly what he was saying. In the distance, he spied a truck driving toward him. Though his cowboy hat shielded him from the hot, early April sun, he still couldn't quite make out whose truck it was. He pressed his finger and thumb against his eyebrows for an added shield, then smiled as the white vehicle came nearer.

Jake stopped the truck and hopped out. They shook hands, and Jake said, "Your dad told me I'd find you out here. Betty make another escape?"

The cow mooed again, and Holden shook his head. "Nope, but if we hadn't caught the near break in this fence when we did, I'm sure she would have."

Jake crossed his arms and leaned against the truck. "So, how you doing? Seems like forever since we've had time to talk."

"We just worked with the boys at church on Wednesday."

Jake swatted the air. "I know, but we're so busy on Wednesday nights."

Holden tilted his head. "You mean you're busy picking up Megan and Vince and then running them back home afterward."

Jake's cheeks darkened. "I suppose that's true."

"So, how are things going with your kindergarten crush?"

"A lot better than they did in kindergarten." They guffawed, then Jake uncrossed his arms and slid his hands in his jeans pockets. "No, really. I care about her. A lot. And I think she cares about me, too."

"That's great. I'm happy for you, man."

"So, anything going on with you and Ava?"

Holden pursed his lips and shook his head. He hadn't tried to contact her since their lunch at the pizza place. He'd fought with himself, lain awake at night, sent more petitions to God than he ever had before, worrying over how to get Ava to talk to him. In the back of his mind, he thought if he gave her some space, a little time, that she'd call or come by and see him. She hadn't. "Nope. Guess not."

"I'm sorry, man." Jake scratched his jaw. "What about that girl from town, the one who works at the bank? Why don't you ask her out?"

Holden curled his lip. "Nah. I think I'm just going to focus on the ranch right now."

Jake nodded. "I understand." He reached into the cab of the truck and pulled out an envelope. "For you."

Holden took it and tore off the flap. "What is it?"

"Reason I came."

Holden pulled out the white parchment with formal embossed silver writing. He read the invitation and his jaw dropped. He looked up at Jake. "You kidding?"

"Nope."

Holden gripped the front of his cowboy hat, lifted it off his head, then wiped the sweat from his brow. "I can't believe this. It's so soon."

Jake nodded. "It sure is, but if I remember right, you called it."

Holden placed the hat back on his head. "That I did."

"I brought it over here to try to help out on the cost. I mean, I know it's just a stamp, but…"

"I still can't believe this is real."

"I have to get fitted for a tux next week. He asked me to be his best man." Jake snarled and spread his arms. "I barely know the guy. I think Jess made him ask me."

Holden burst out laughing. "I can't believe your little sister is getting married before both of us."

His friend rolled his eyes. "Ugh. It's all she and Mom talk about. Colors and cakes and dresses and flowers. Dad and I are about to die." He leaned forward. "And do you know how much a cake costs?"

Holden shook his head as he tried to contain his mirth.

"Let's just say it's ridiculous. A downright rip-off is what it is. I'm all for Megan and me just heading to the courthouse."

Holden lifted his chin. "Sounds like you care about her more than just a little bit."

Jake shrugged. "I might."

Holden lifted up the envelope. "Thanks for the invite.

You can tell your family I'll be there. Might even whoop and holler as she walks down the aisle."

"Don't you dare. Jess is all bent out of shape trying to make it the 'event of the year'." He growled. "I'm telling ya, the women in my house are crazy right now."

Jake's smartphone rang and he pulled it out of his jeans. He grinned. "It's Megan. I'll see you later."

Holden watched as his friend drove away. He pulled the invitation out of the envelope again. Little Jess Thomas was getting married. The girl had driven him and Jake crazy growing up. Messed with their army men. Interrupted their games. Now, she was going to commit herself to a man for the rest of her life.

He looked at the dust stirred up by Jake's departure. His best friend was also in love. Holden wanted to be happy for both of them, but his heart ached for Ava.

Ava picked up a plump red pepper and handed it to Aunt Irene for inspection. "I still don't understand why I have to go."

Aunt Irene smelled the vegetable before adding it to the bulging plastic bag. "Because Jerry and I have a surprise for you."

"Isn't it Jerry's birthday dinner? Why would you have a surprise for me?"

She lifted her right shoulder. "Actually, we have a surprise for you and my boys and his kids."

Ava placed her hand on her aunt's forearm. "You're not…surely, you two aren't getting married."

Aunt Irene giggled as she pressed her palm against her chest. "Why, heaven's no. We aren't even dating."

Ava crossed her arms in front of her and pursed her lips.

Her aunt took a step back. "It's true. We haven't gone

on one real date." She twirled her hand. "I suppose I have to admit we've spent a good deal of time together, and it's true we enjoy each other's company." She cupped her chin. "What was my argument again?"

"That you and Jerry aren't dating."

"That's right." She lifted her hands. "We're not."

"But you're cooking dinner for his birthday?"

"Yes."

"For his entire family and your entire family?"

Aunt Irene nodded.

"To eat together?"

Aunt Irene placed her palm on her hip. "What is your point, Ava?"

She lifted her brows and shrugged. "I don't know. Sounds like you're dating to me."

Aunt Irene lifted the bag. "I've got ten peppers. That'll make twenty stuffed peppers." She started counting on her fingers. "Let's see, Jerry has six people in his family. Him and Holden. The two girls and their husbands."

"And we have four," added Ava.

"Hmm. That's ten people, and the men might want more than two peppers."

"What exactly are you making?"

Aunt Irene dug her smartphone out of her purse. "I found this really cool app here."

Ava wrinkled her nose. "It sounds weird to hear my sixty-year-old aunt talk all techie."

Irene tilted the phone. "I love this little device. I'm so glad Matt talked me into joining the twenty-first century, as he likes to say. Anyway, I have all these really neat recipes to help people with high blood pressure."

"That's great."

"Yes. We're going to have quinoa and black bean stuffed peppers."

"What's quinoa?"

"It's a seed. Full of protein and fiber. Very healthy."

Ava scrunched up her face. "Sounds yummy."

"It will be. You'll see."

"I'm just teasing. Everything you cook is delicious."

Aunt Irene selected a couple more peppers, then grabbed a package of carrots and a few onions. They'd made their way to the next aisle when Ava stopped, blinking at the couple in front of her. "Mitch?"

Mitch and a red-haired woman turned around. "Mom? Ava? What are you doing here?"

"Getting groceries. What are you doing?" asked Ava. She took in the woman's short red hair, bright green eyes and freckles, and such a beaming smile that Ava had to smile back.

He cleared his throat. "Picking up some steak sauce."

Aunt Irene reached over and grabbed the woman's hand. "I'm Mitch's mother, Irene. It's a pleasure to meet you."

"I'm Ellie." The woman accepted the handshake with fervor, then shook Ava's hand as well. She looked up at Mitch and batted her eyelids. "I'm so glad to meet you. Mitchy planned to see if we could all get together next week, but I've been so anxious to meet his family."

To Ava's surprise, Mitch's expression softened more with each word she said. Ellie grabbed his hand and he actually held it.

Excitement shone on Irene's face as she wrapped Ellie in a hug. "I'm sorry we ruined the surprise, but I'm so glad we met."

"How long have you been dating?" asked Ava.

"It'll be two months tomorrow." Ellie placed her palm against Mitch's chest. "Right, Mitchy?"

So, he was dating her before I came back to Surprise,

and he never mentioned it. The rascal. Ellie seemed sweet and perky, a direct contrast to her most-of-the-time-negative cousin.

Ava and Holden were different, as well. A physical therapist and a cowboy rancher. He liked casual, and she liked fashion. She blinked. Why had she thought of Holden? She'd done well the last few weeks, forbidding the man to traipse through her thoughts.

Irene motioned toward their cart. "Tomorrow night I'm fixing dinner for one of my dear friends and his family. Ellie, I'd love for you to come."

She giggled. "That would be great. Right, Mitchy?"

He nodded, and they said goodbye. Once Mitch and Ellie were out of sight, Ava turned to her aunt. "Did you know he was dating?"

Irene seemed as perplexed as she was. "Not a clue."

"I think he likes her."

"Me, too."

"She seems really sweet." Ava bit her bottom lip. "Different than the girl I would have envisioned for Mitch."

"You mean 'cause she's happy?"

Ava chuckled. "You gotta admit Mitch tends be a bit of a grump."

"Oh, I know he's a half-empty glass. He's been that way all his life." Irene's lips curved into a smile. "That girl is good for him."

"Maybe they'll settle down quick and start giving you grandbabies." Ava's heart beat faster as soon as the words left her mouth.

Irene snorted. "Don't even tease, Ava. What I wouldn't give to have a little one running around the house."

Tears welled in Ava's eyes, and she turned toward the shelves. She picked up several cans of unsalted black beans and placed them in the cart. "The recipe said you need cumin powder. I'll go get it."

She didn't have to look at her aunt. She could feel Aunt Irene's compassion and pity. Ava dabbed the corners of her eyes and forbade her mind to wander.

Chapter 9

Holden pushed the food around with his fork. Irene was a good cook, but he didn't like peppers, and he didn't know what to think about the seedy looking things inside them. He was glad she wanted to help his dad keep his blood pressure down, but some of the recipes she came up with were not his favorites.

He looked around the table. Six people from his family. Five from Irene's. All sitting at their humongous table celebrating his dad's birthday. But Holden didn't feel celebratory.

His dad and Irene sat side by side, quietly sharing snippets about their day and laughing intermittently. His sister Sara and brother-in-law Daryl sat next to them, then his other sister, Traci, and her husband, Carl. Mitch and Ellie sat next to them. Their ooey-gooey expressions toward each other made Holden's stomach churn. Next around the table was Ava, himself, then Matt. Somehow, he'd ended up seated between the woman he couldn't stop thinking about, and her cousin.

Holden picked through the pepper and speared a couple black beans. Ava looked awfully pretty tonight, wearing a blue flowered dress that made her eyes look amazing, and she smelled so good. Like sunshine and flowers.

He wished she would talk to him. Everyone he knew seemed to be finding love. Jess and Nate. Jake and Megan. Dad and Irene. Even Mitch. Mitch was the last person in Surprise Holden would expect to find a girlfriend, and yet here he was, sitting next to a spunky redhead who looked at him as if he hung the moon.

Holden wasn't accomplishing anything just sitting and stewing about his lack of a love life. Today was his dad's birthday, so he might as well try and make the best of it. He turned toward Matt. "So, how are things going?"

Matt wiped his mouth. "Really well. We just finished making repairs on a few homes in the downtown area. Getting ready for our Easter pageant."

"That's great."

"Yes. We're hoping to have a thousand people attend. The kids have been passing out flyers."

His phone beeped, and Matt pulled it out of his pocket. He smiled as he opened a text from someone named Barb. Holden leaned back in his chair. Even Matt seemed to have found himself a girl.

This is crazy. Ava might have decided to avoid him, but Holden was not going to be part of it. They'd made a mistake when they were barely adults. God had forgiven them, and even if she wanted nothing to do with him, he planned to talk to her and treat her as he would anyone else.

He looked her way. She gazed into his eyes, her expression timid and vulnerable. The only problem with treating her like anyone else was he could never think of her that way. She would always mean much more to him. He blew out a quick breath, determined not to drown in the beauty of those eyes. "How is work going?"

She swallowed, and Holden had to look away from her mouth and neck. "Great. How 'bout you?"

"Same as always."

He twirled the fork between his thumb and fingers. What else could he say to her? She wouldn't appreciate him sharing that he thought of her constantly and that he was pretty sure he loved her as much as he had eight years ago. No. Those were not sentiments Ava would want to hear.

Irene tapped her fork against a glass of water, and everyone looked toward her and Dad. "Before the cake and ice cream, Jerry and I have a little announcement to make."

Surely they're not going to say they're getting married. Holden wanted his dad to be happy, and he seemed more alive than he had in years, but he and Irene hadn't spent enough time together as a couple. Not really. They'd known each other for ages, and they probably didn't need as much get-to-know-each-other time as most, but still.

"We have decided…" Irene glanced at his dad. "Do you want to tell them?"

He shook his head. "You go ahead."

"We're going to sing a duet in Senior Idol."

Laughter burst out around the room, and Irene scrunched her face. "What's so funny?"

"We thought you were going to say you're engaged," said Mitch.

She pressed her palm against her chest. "Jerry hasn't even taken me on the first date."

Dad scratched his jaw. "I suppose I haven't." He snapped his fingers. "Well, that's going to have to change. Irene, how would you like to go out with me tomorrow night?"

She giggled. "Sure." Then she elbowed his arm. "Do I get to pick the movie?"

"Of course. As long as I get to pick the restaurant."

Irene shook his hand. "Deal." She turned back toward them. "We're going to give you a preview of our song tonight."

Cheers erupted, and Holden's heart warmed at the pleasure that spread over his dad's face. He also noted that each day spent with Irene seemed to make his dad more energetic and youthful.

Dad gestured around the table. "So, let's finish up and get these dishes out of the way."

Holden stood and started clearing the table. He carried a pile of dishes into the kitchen and scraped the excess food into the trash. After plugging the sink, he turned on the hot water, added soap and started washing. A few minutes later Ava stood beside him. "I don't mind helping."

He nodded. "Why don't you take over washing, and I'll dry and put away?"

She agreed. They worked in silence, and Holden fought the urge to ask her out again. His dad always said he was stubborn as an old mule when it came to the things he wanted. And Holden wanted Ava.

"We make a good team." Ava's voice was quiet.

"I always thought so."

She opened her mouth, but before she could speak, Irene hollered for everyone to join them in the living room. Holden grabbed a couple dining room chairs and carried them there for him and Ava. His dad stood holding a microphone connected to a portable karaoke machine, a sight Holden had never imagined seeing. And yet his dad didn't seem the slightest bit worried about singing with Irene in front of everybody.

She pushed the play button and a country tune filled the room. Within moments, Irene and Dad were singing the lyrics of "Islands in the Stream." They sounded terrific together. When the song ended, both families erupted in applause.

"You two are gonna win for sure," said Mitch's girlfriend.

"Dad, I didn't know you could sing," declared Sara.

"No kidding," added Traci. "You've got some pipes."

He shrugged. "I suppose sometimes there's more to a person than you realize."

Holden glanced at Ava. There was definitely something more to her, something that made her run from him. He knew she had feelings for him. At least he believed she did, but for some reason she refused to give them a chance.

Ava opened the file drawer and pulled out a list of hip exercises to give to her patient. She found a few brochures and scooped them up, as well.

"Do you have plans later?" asked Katie.

Ava shook her head. The nineteen-year-old had recently cut her long dark hair into shoulder-length layers. The more mature style looked good on her. "Not really. Just a quick dinner and some TV time."

"I need to go to the mall and find a dress for Easter." She twirled a pen between her fingers. "I'm meeting Corey's parents this weekend."

Ava lifted her eyebrows. "Really?"

"And I'm a little nervous. They have a big dinner with extended family and everything after church."

"You'll be fine. They'll love you."

"I hope so." She tapped the pen against the desk. "You think you could go to the mall with me?"

"Sure. I might look for a new dress, as well."

"Terrific."

"I have one more appointment, then I'll be ready."

Ava walked back to the room and finished exercises with

the patient. She was glad to have something to keep her busy tonight. Since Jerry's birthday dinner, she'd dreamed of Holden twice. Aunt Irene and Jerry would be going on their big movie date tonight, and though she was happy for her aunt, she didn't want to be a bystander to their budding romance. Not every day, anyway. A distraction was welcome.

Once at the mall, Katie led her through shop after shop, trying on one dress after another. Despite being in good shape, Ava eventually found that her feet hurt, and she was ready to settle down and eat some dinner.

Katie hefted her purse higher onto her shoulder. "It's hopeless. I'm never going to find the right dress."

Ava pointed to a small, locally-owned boutique tucked in a corner of the mall. "Let's try in here."

She pouted. "They never have anything, and their prices are ridiculous."

"You never know. Maybe they're having a sale." Ava looped her arm with Katie's. "If we don't find anything, we'll have some dinner, then try a few places on the other side of town."

They walked into the store, and Ava nodded a greeting to the clerk. *Please, let us find a dress.* They headed to a rack toward the back of the shop that was stuffed with bright-colored gowns. Ava unhooked a gold dress that cinched in at the waist and flowed down in layers to just below the knees. "Look at this one. It would look beautiful with your skin tone and hair color."

Katie shrugged. "It's sorta pretty. I'd need to try it on."

Ava handed her the gown, then searched through more dresses. She found a red one and an orange one and gave them to Katie. The teen didn't seem thrilled with any of the options, but agreed to try them on.

Ava continued to look through the rack until she spied a purple dress with spaghetti straps. The bust was pleated above a cinched waist, with a full skirt stopping just above the knee. Something about the light cotton material and simple design drew Ava. She lifted the hanger off the rack.

Katie oohed. "That would look so good on you."

"You think so?" Ava pressed the dress against her chest. She thought of Holden and how he always complimented her when she wore purple. Realizing what she was thinking, she blinked and hooked the dress back on the rack. She didn't want to consider things Holden would like.

"What are you doing?" Katie pulled the dress out again. "You're trying this on." She lifted the gold dress. "If I'm trying this, you're trying that."

Ava grinned as she took the purple dress from Katie's hand. "Fine. But let's get to it. I'm hungry."

They made their way to the dressing rooms. Ava put on the purple dress and gazed at her reflection. A terrific fit. Complimented her shape. Felt comfortable. She looked at the tag. And not a terrible price. Maybe a bit more than she would normally spend, but not too much.

"I can't believe it," Katie said from the next cubicle.

Ava stepped out of her room. "What?"

"This dress is absolutely beautiful." She scurried out in turn and twirled in front of Ava. "I never would have picked this."

The gold color complimented Katie's hair and skin just as Ava had predicted, and the design gave her a fun, but mature appearance. "You look beautiful."

Katie touched her earlobes. "I'll just get a pair of dangly gold earrings. Maybe an oversize gold ring or bracelet."

"Now you're talking my department."

Katie giggled. "You do wear the cutest jewelry." She gasped and pointed at Ava. "I love that dress on you. Please tell me you're going to buy it."

Ava nodded. "I think I am."

They changed back into their clothes, purchased the dresses, then made one last stop at a fashion jewelry store to pick up accessories. Katie finally rubbed her stomach. "I'm starving."

"Me, too. How about Italian?"

The teen nodded and they walked to the restaurant beside the mall. Once they were seated and had ordered their food, Katie took a sip of her water with extra lemon. "I've talked so much about me and Corey that I've never asked if you have a boyfriend."

Ava shook her head. "Nope."

Katie scrunched her nose. "Not even someone you're interested in?"

She pursed her lips. "Not really." Her cheeks warmed with the untruth of her words.

"Come on. There's gotta be someone."

Ava released a breath. "There is a guy I cared a lot about years ago."

"From your hometown?"

"No. From Surprise."

Katie sat up straighter. "Really? Have you seen him since you moved back here?"

"Yes." Ava clasped her hands under the table and rubbed her thumbs against her palms.

"He's not married or anything, is he?"

"No. He's single."

Katie waved. "Then look him up. See if you can get together." She winked. "Maybe reignite an old flame."

"He's asked me to dinner a few times, but…"

"But what? He still means something to you if you brought him up to me."

Ava rubbed her hands together. "It's not that simple. We had a bad breakup. A lot of unresolved issues."

Katie smacked the table and leaned forward. "Aren't

you the one who told me not to run away from my problems?" She lifted her fist. "But to face them head-on?"

Ava nodded. She needed to do just that, to fess up the whole truth to Holden. She'd feel better. In her spirit, God urged her to go ahead and lay the past out there. The good, the bad, and the ugly.

But then she pictured Holden's expression when he found out all she'd kept from him. She'd be the cause of so much pain.

The truth will set you free.

She'd be set free, but what about Holden? He'd be devastated. If she'd talked to him eight years ago, everything would be different. Now, the truth would only cause him pain. No. It was better if he never knew.

Chapter 10

Holden flipped his wrist, casting the hook and bait a good ways into the lake. "One of these days we're going to have to pick a different place to fish."

With his line already cast, Jake settled into a collapsible fishing chair. "What are you talking about? This is tradition. We've been coming to Surprise Lake the day before Easter for as long as I can remember."

Holden nodded to the father and son duo setting up their fishing gear a few yards away, then looked to his other side at the couple of older guys settled in beside them, closer than Holden would have preferred. "Yeah, but the lake's getting a little crowded."

Jake clicked his tongue. "Few people never hurt nothing."

"We could easily fish on my land."

Jake pointed to the ground. "But this is tradition."

Holden chuckled. "I'm fine if you're fine. Just seems a little silly that we can only keep four catfish apiece when we fish here, when we can keep as many as we want from the ranch. We always buy more for Dad to fry up."

Jake lifted his brows and grinned. "Tradition."

"Hey, boys."

Holden turned and saw his father walking toward them, carrying his chair and fishing gear. "Dad, I didn't think you were going to make it this year."

He plopped his stuff down beside Holden, then wiped his brow with a handkerchief. "I didn't think so, either. Irene's got me learning moves to go along with the song for Senior Idol." He shook his head and mumbled under his breath.

Jake crowed. "Jerry Whitaker dancing. I can't wait to see this."

Dad lifted his pointer finger. "It ain't dancing. It's just moves." He pointed to his chest. "That woman can talk me into a lot of things, but dancing ain't one of them."

"Your dad's got a girlfriend." Jake nudged Holden's shoulder and laughed. "I never thought I'd see the day."

Holden bit the inside of his cheek and watched as his father baited the hook and cast the line. He never thought he'd see the day, either. Irene was a terrific woman, and he was glad Dad had found someone to care about, but the whole thing still seemed strange. Even though his mother had been gone since Holden was knee-high to Dad, and she'd passed away not too many years after that, the thought of his dad and dating had never gone together in his mind.

"Never thought I would, either." After sitting down, Dad shoved a piece of licorice in his mouth. "Expected to grow old alone."

Jake whistled. "Hmm. Are you saying you don't plan to grow old alone now? Are you thinking long-term?"

Dad shrugged as a silly sideways grin spread his lips.

Holden looked across the lake. Parents and grandparents were setting up all around them, with children of various ages and sizes. A young man and a very pregnant woman walked a small terrier on the dog trail that went around part of the lake.

Though it was early in the morning, the air was already warm. Supposed to be ninety degrees by afternoon. He lifted his cowboy hat and wiped perspiration from his forehead with the back of his hand. He was tired of thinking about happy couples and families and kids.

His dad spat on the ground. "What are you teasing me for, Jakey boy? I believe you have a love interest, as well."

Jake smiled as he folded his hands together behind his head. "That I do."

"You and Megan getting serious?" he asked.

Holden touched his pole, then looked at Jake's and his dad's. Couldn't just one fish latch on to one of their baits so they could stop talking about women? Jake was determined to keep up tradition, but to Holden's recollection the yearly fishing trip to Surprise Lake the day before Easter never included discussions about girls. In fact, when they were younger the mention of the female population had been expressly forbidden.

"I'd reckon," responded Jake. "We're getting married."

Holden and his dad sat forward and looked at him at the same time. "What?" they said in unison.

Jake laughed as he smacked the top of his knee. "You heard me right. She's agreed to marry me."

Holden furrowed his brows. "What about Jess and her wedding?"

"I don't suppose me getting married has anything to do with my sister."

"But you said your mom and sister were going nuts with plans for Jess's wedding. Your mom'll be fit to be tied."

Holden recalled Jake's mother from when they were kids. The woman went berserk anytime something unexpected or overwhelming happened. Holden especially remembered the time Jake ran into the house, his head bleeding all over the place because he'd fallen out of a tree, and his mom had fainted. Literally passed out flat on the floor. Holden and Jess had to clean Jake up before their mom finally came to.

"Well, we're not getting married at the same time. In fact, Megan and I decided not to have a formal gathering. We're just going to have Vince and our immediate families at the church to exchange vows. No reception or nothing."

"So your parents don't mind that the two of you are getting married so close together? Your mom especially?" asked Dad.

Holden didn't look at his father; he'd burst out laughing if he did. Dad knew Jake's mom to be a little tightly wound. She'd had a conniption fit once when he and Jake got into a tussle when they were boys. Nobody was hurt, and both of them faced discipline from their daddies, but Jake's mom had had a hard time getting past the incident.

"Why, they're happier than a rooster in a henhouse. They've already taken Vince on as their grandson and are hinting for us to add a few more as soon as possible."

Holden swallowed back the shock. Jake and Jess were getting married, and Jake was even talking about babies.

Dad stood, walked over to him and extended his hand. "I'm happy for you, son."

Jake hopped out of his chair and grabbed him in a hug. "You can do better than that."

They both chuckled as they patted each other's back, and Dad offered his congratulations.

Holden stood on heavy legs as he hugged his best friend in turn. "Congratulations, man."

Jake gave Holden a fistbump. "Thanks. I'm still praying she'll come around."

Holden pretended not to hear that as he released his friend and sat back in his chair. He didn't want to think about Ava. Jake jabbered about his and Megan's plans, and Holden tapped the fishing pole again. He glanced around them. Most everyone had caught at least one fish, but they hadn't gotten even a nibble.

While Jake continued to talk, Holden focused on his boots. They were scuffed quite a bit at the toe, and the leather looked pretty worn. Comfortable, true, but maybe it was time for a new pair. He moved his feet. No. He liked these boots. No reason to go searching for a new pair when these fit him just fine.

Ava's face floated through his mind. *That's the problem, God. When something or someone fits, you just wanna keep 'em. Ava fit me just right, and I gotta figure out a way to get her back.*

"Did you hear Jerry telling me about Holden?"

Ava adjusted the thin white belt around her waist. Though she'd berated herself several times, she'd been disappointed when Holden wasn't at church for Easter Sunday. Not that she wanted him to notice her. She didn't. Or at least she didn't *want* to want that. Still, she'd hoped to see a glimmer of approval in his eyes.

Deep in her heart, she couldn't deny the purple dress was for him. She'd added a thin white belt, white stone earrings and bracelet, and sandals with white ribbons that tied around her ankles. Extra effort had been given to her hair and makeup. But he wasn't there. "What did Jerry say?"

"Apparently, he sprained his ankle badly yesterday, getting on or off the tractor." Aunt Irene placed the roast on the counter. "Can't remember which he said."

Ava took down plates for the family, then set the table. "I hope he's all right."

"They thought he broke it. Took him to get X-rays, but it was just a sprain. Supposed to stay off it for two weeks minimum, but I doubt he will."

Ava set out the plates, silverware and napkins. She stirred the mashed potatoes, then took the rolls out of the pantry. As much time as they spent together, she'd expected Jerry and Aunt Irene to want to share Easter dinner. With both families. But her aunt hadn't mentioned it, and Ava had been relieved.

Aunt Irene took the rolls from her hands. "I'll butter them. Why don't you give your mom and dad a call before the boys and Ellie get here?"

Ava grabbed her smartphone off the counter and walked into the living room. As she scrolled through her contacts, she released a sigh. She'd moved to Surprise seven weeks ago, the last week of February, and she'd talked to her parents only a handful of times. Each time, she'd been the one to call them.

Trying her dad's number first, since he was most likely to answer, she waited through the rings until his voice mail picked up. After leaving a message, she tried her mom's number.

"Hello."

Ava sat up straighter. "Hi, Mom."

"Hello, Ava. You sound surprised."

"I just didn't expect you to answer." She bit her lip, realizing, true or not, that the words didn't sound nice.

"Well, you know how busy your dad and I are."

Ava nodded. "I do. So, how are you?"

"We're good. Dad's sitting beside me. He says hello. We're heading to lunch. How are you?"

"Good." Ava searched her thoughts for something to

say. She and her parents had never been close, but even casual conversation had become strained after she'd left Surprise eight years ago. "I love my job here. The family I work for have really taken me under their wing."

"That's good. And how's Irene?"

"She's great. Has a boyfriend."

"Oh my." Her voice sounded distant, and Ava knew her mom wasn't really listening. "Turn here, dear," she whispered, most likely to Ava's dad. "Well, we're almost to the restaurant, Ava. Have a good day."

"Happy Easter, Mom."

"Oh, yes, yes. Happy Easter. Dad says to tell you we love you."

Ava pursed her lips. "Love you, too."

She pushed the end button, then set the phone on the couch beside her. Staring at a picture on the wall, of a Mexican family gathered together at a table for an afternoon meal, she tried to empty her mind of all thoughts. Not an easy task. Especially at this time of year.

"They're busy, huh?"

Ava turned and saw Aunt Irene wiping her hands on a white apron with Kiss the Cook embroidered on it. Ava shrugged. "Like always."

Her aunt walked around the couch, sat beside her and patted her leg. "I don't know why they don't take some time to smell the roses."

Ava grinned. "They've always been busy. Go-getters, Dad likes to say. I had everything I wanted, and often the very best, but they weren't around much."

"They do love you."

Ava twisted the bracelet around her wrist. "You know, I think they do, but..."

"They don't know how."

She shifted to face her aunt. "But why? You're one of

the most loving mothers I know, and I've seen the pictures of you and Dad growing up. Your family was close."

"Yes, but your mom was passed from one home to the other. She'd been neglected, and I think she just doesn't know how to show love. Providing for you is her way of telling you."

Ava closed her eyes. Most of her life she'd avoided getting too close to people. Not that she didn't enjoy them. She had a care and concern for others that must have come directly from God, but aside from Aunt Irene, Ava feared allowing herself to truly open up and love. Which was why her feelings for Holden had been so terrifying. Why the upcoming week would be so hard.

"Seven years this week, huh?" Aunt Irene whispered.

Tears welled in her eyes as she nodded. Aunt Irene wrapped her hand around Ava's head and pressed her face into her shoulder. Ava was helpless to stop the tears as they fell.

Her aunt held her and cooed whispers of reassurance, while Ava tried to breathe against the weight that pressed on her chest. From experience, she knew the deep-to-the-core sadness would pass in a week or so. But she could never forget.

Chapter 11

Holden limped into the Miller Physical Therapy Clinic building. Even held the crutches under his armpits for added support. His ankle still smarted, no doubt about that, but normally, he'd just wrap it up good and tight and keep right on working. This wasn't normal circumstances. The only way he'd be able to see Ava was if she was forced to see him.

After opening the front door, he looked around. Nice lobby. Contemporary brown leather chairs. Bright, desert-themed artwork on the walls. He'd heard good things about the Millers. Knew they ran a Christian office. Noting the picture quoting a Psalm above the receptionist's desk, he read, "The Lord makes firm the steps of the one who delights in him."

The young, dark-haired girl looked up at him, then turned back toward the picture. "Oh, yeah. Dad had that made."

"Quite fitting for a physical therapy office."

She pointed to the sign-in sheet. "Sure is."

He signed his name. "So, you're Rick and Mary Miller's daughter?"

"Yep." She handed him a clipboard containing information forms, then turned to the computer. "I'll just need to see your insurance card, and I'll get you set up here. Ava will be with you in just a few minutes."

He gave her the card and took the clipboard. After taking a seat, he frowned at the stack of pages he had to fill out. He was not a fan of going to the doctor, and especially didn't like divulging every tidbit of personal information they all seemed determined to know. He turned up his lip. *Now, why do they want to know if anyone in my family's had cancer? I'm just here for a sprained ankle.*

He sighed and finished the pages. People were there for more reasons than just sprained ankles, he knew. The Millers probably had their reasons for asking. Once finished, he took the clipboard back to the receptionist, then sat back down.

God, give me the right words to say. Nothing heavy. Just help me let her work on my ankle, and not do anything to make her uncomfortable.

Ava stood in the doorway leading back to the rehabilitation rooms. She saw him and her eyes widened in surprise. She reached for the clipboard he'd just given to the dark-haired girl. "He's my next patient?"

The girl nodded. "Holden Whitaker."

Ava swallowed as she looked back at him. Her hands shook just a tad as she motioned for him to follow her. He limped back to the room, and she shut the door behind them. He hadn't thought about being alone with her. How he wished he could just scoop her up in his arms and smother her with kisses.

He settled in one of the chairs, and she sat on a stool.

"Aunt Irene mentioned you'd sprained your ankle a few days ago."

Holden nodded. "Yep. Getting off the tractor. My left leg snagged on the corner of the seat, and before I could catch myself my right foot twisted and my ankle popped."

She read through his charts. "Looks like your doctor said physical therapy was an option."

He clasped his hands together. "And I'm opting to take it."

A knowing grin spread over her lips. "With me?"

"Gotta have the best."

"And I'm the best?"

"To me, you are."

Ava glanced back down at the chart, and Holden inwardly berated himself. He needed to keep their time together easy. Wanted her to feel comfortable with him again.

She placed the clipboard on a small table. "Okay. Well, the first thing you're going to have to do is take off your cowboy boot and sock."

"Are you kidding?"

Ava chuckled. "How else are we going to strengthen the ankle?"

He reached down and pulled them off. "Don't say I didn't warn you."

Ava wrinkled her nose, and Holden felt heat wash down his neck and back. She tapped his leg. "I'm just kidding."

She unrolled the wrapping, then studied both sides of the bruised ankle. "You sprained it pretty good."

"Told ya."

"I'm surprised you're not just trying to walk it off."

He pointed to the paper. "You read it. Doc said I might need therapy two or three times a week."

"I did, and I'm glad you're doing this right. No need in

having trouble with your ankle years down the road because you didn't allow it to heal properly now."

"I agree."

She placed his foot on the floor. "Okay. The first thing I want you to do is trace the alphabet with your toes. This allows the ankle to move in every direction."

Holden did as she said. By the time he'd gotten halfway through, his ankle throbbed, but he kept going. "You like working here?"

"I love it. The Millers are wonderful people."

He traced the *Z* and leaned back in the chair, the soreness more than he'd anticipated. "I've heard good things about them."

She patted his knee. "I want you to do it again."

Ignoring the discomfort, he obeyed her every command, and talked to her about everything he could think of. He shared news about the ranch and about Betty constantly trying to find ways of escape. He told Ava about catching Dad and Irene doing some kind of moves in the living room. She shared about finding a big, yellow wig in her aunt's room.

"Do you think they're going to dress up like Dolly Parton and Kenny Rogers?" Holden asked.

Ava giggled. "I think so."

She wrapped both hands around his foot, and Holden's heartbeat raced. She moved it forward and back with strength and confidence, then placed it back on the ground and instructed him on another exercise.

"You really do a great job, Ava."

She raised her eyebrows. "You think so, huh?"

He pointed to his throbbing ankle. "I can feel it."

Ava laughed, an unrestrained sound that he hadn't heard in almost eight years. She gave him a few sheets of paper. "These are exercises you need to do at home."

He folded and stuck them in his back pocket. If those exercises helped heal his ankle he wouldn't do a single one.

Ava walked out of the room, and he limped behind her. Once back in the lobby, he said, "I'll see you in a couple days."

She grinned. "Okay. It was good talking with you, Holden."

He made his way back to the truck, hopped into the cab, then leaned his head back and closed his eyes. His ankle throbbed, but he didn't mind a bit. "Thank you, Lord, for a sprained ankle."

Ava grabbed her purse out of the cabinet. Aunt Irene had another date with Jerry, so Ava planned to grab a salad and head over to the White Tanks. She hadn't expected to see Holden, even though they'd had a good session and a nice time talking, too. Now she needed to walk, spend some time with God in nature, and think. Actually, sometimes she wondered if she did a bit too much thinking.

"That Holden guy was cute with a capital *C*." Katie bit down on the top of her pen.

Ava dug through her purse in search of her keys. "He's handsome."

"I got a feeling you already knew the guy."

"I did."

"And unless I'm blind, and I'm not, I think the guy might be a little interested in you."

Ava looked up and narrowed her gaze.

Katie lifted her hand and squeezed her thumb and finger together. "Just a little bit."

Ava couldn't help but smile. "He's the guy I told you about."

The teen pressed her palms against the desk and sat

forward, eyes wide with interest. "The one you ran away from?"

She nodded.

Katie motioned to the door. "Well, go after him. I'm telling you, the guy's still got a thing for you." She leaned back in her chair and lifted her face toward the ceiling. "And he's so cute."

"And you're so dramatic." Ava tapped the edge of the desk. "I'll see you tomorrow."

"Suit yourself, but someone's gonna snatch up that guy."

Ava picked up some dinner, then drove to the mountains. The weather was definitely starting to get hot. Ninety degrees, but she didn't care. She needed to walk, to be alone. After parking the car, she sat at a nearby picnic table and ate her dinner. Once finished, she tied her hair in a ponytail and grabbed a bottle of water out of the backseat.

She walked her favorite trail, drinking in the colorful wildflowers, with the mountains reaching to the heavens in the background. She quickened her pace until her chest burned from the exertion. Still she kept going.

The air was hot, and strands of hair clung to her face as she started to perspire. Her muscles tightened and her heart pounded, and soon her shirt was wet with sweat. Spying a large rock a little ways ahead, she started to run, to sprint until she reached it. Flopping onto the rock, she opened the water bottle and chugged a long drink.

Gasping to catch her breath, she leaned back on the rock and released a low howl. "Whew. That felt good."

She leaned forward again, placed her elbows on her knees and dipped her chin. She blew down her shirt to cool herself, then took another drink of water.

Katie's words, *someone's gonna snatch up that guy*, raced through her mind. Ava didn't want that to happen. In only a thirty-minute session, she'd realized just how much she did not want it to. They'd talked about everything and nothing, and the conversation had felt right. She remembered afresh why she'd fallen in love with Holden as a young woman. Not only was he gorgeous, but she genuinely enjoyed his company.

Her mind wandered to eight years ago, and she shook her head and lifted her face to the sky. "No thinking about the past." With the statement came the urge to scream at the top of her lungs. She opened her arms wide. "No thinking about the past. I can't change it, anyway."

She looked down the trail, and her stomach tightened when she saw an older couple walking toward her. When they passed, the woman winked. "You're absolutely right, honey. Need to just keep looking ahead."

Ava waved despite the embarrassment that washed through her. Trekking back to the car, she drove home with the windows down, allowing the hot wind to whip through her hair. Throughout the night, any time her mind tried to wander, she envisioned the woman telling her to look ahead.

The next morning she headed into work and stopped at the bouquet of wildflowers sitting on Katie's desk—lupines and poppies, with a big purple ribbon tied around the vase. Ava's favorite flowers. Her favorite color. Her heart pounded against her chest. "Corey buy you flowers?"

Katie shook her head. "Nope. They're for you."

Ava opened the card and read, "Thanks for being a great physical therapist. Holden."

"From Mr. Good-looking yesterday?" asked Katie.

She grinned. "Maybe."

The teen waved a pen back and forth. "I'm telling you, Ava. He's entirely too cute, and you said he was a Christian to boot."

She lifted her hand to stop Katie from saying more. "I'm not going to let anything happen to him."

Katie leaned forward. "Does that mean what I think it means?"

Ava looked at the clock on the desk and tilted her head. "If you think it means it's time to get to work, then you're right."

Katie swatted the air. "Fine. Don't tell me anything."

Ava laughed as she put her purse in the cabinet, then looked over her schedule. Today would be a good day.

Chapter 12

Three weeks had passed since Holden started going to physical therapy. Ava had lightened up, and they'd enjoyed many conversations. She'd shared some of the interesting experiences she'd had during college and training, and he told her things he'd learned on the ranch.

Today she'd opened up about her dream to go on a mission trip to help people who might never have the chance to have therapy. Her words had resonated in his heart. "It's funny, Holden. I don't even know where I'd go." She'd touched her chest. "I just feel like I'm supposed to."

He leaned against the wall in the church classroom now. *She's finally opening up to me again.* He wanted to ask her out, but had to make sure she was ready.

"You ready, man?"

Jake tapped his arm, and Holden stood up straight. He glanced at the clock on the wall. Five minutes past time to start, and all the regular boys had already made their way into the room. He scratched his jaw. "Guess I better start paying closer attention."

Holden sat down beside the old felt storyboard his teachers had used when he was a kid growing up in the church. He picked up the package containing the felt pieces for the Jonah tale. "Hey, guys, who remembers what story we're going to talk about today?"

Zack jumped up. "You know I'm seven now."

Holden nodded as he motioned for the boy to sit back down. "Yes. I was at your party, remember?"

Zack jutted out his chin. "I'm older than John."

John crossed his arms in front of his chest and let out a huff.

"Zack, I asked about the story. What story from the Bible are we going to talk about today?" asked Holden.

Zack shrugged as he plopped back in his chair.

Vince raised his hand. "We're going to talk about Jonah."

Jake patted Vince's shoulder then lifted his chin. Holden grinned at the pride his friend felt for Megan's son.

"That's right," said Holden. He pulled out the Jonah felt piece and stuck it onto the board. "Jonah was a man of God during his time. He was a prophet." Holden furrowed his brows and scratched his chin. "What is a prophet?"

Zack hopped back up. "It's when you make more money than you spend."

Holden shook his head. "No...well, actually, yes. That is the definition of profit, but I'm talking about when a prophet is a person."

While Jake nudged Zack to sit down again, Sean raised his hand. "It's someone who tells what God is about to do."

Holden nodded. "That's exactly right, and I love the way you described him." He pointed to the board. "God told Jonah to tell the Ninevites to stop being bad and follow God's ways."

He stuck up a felt piece showing a group of people with angry faces. "But Jonah had a problem. Does anyone know what that was?"

"He didn't like the Ninevites," said John. Then he stuck out his tongue at Zack. Zack stuck out his tongue as well, and Jake plopped a chair between them and sat down.

"Yep," Jake said. "He didn't like the Ninevites, so he got on a boat and tried to run away."

Holden placed a boat on the board and stuck Jonah on top of it. "But you know what?"

"You can't run from God," said Zack. "It's like trying to run from the cops. They're gonna catch up with you eventually. My uncle, he found that out the hard way."

Holden almost laughed out loud. His dad would have called that curly haired redhead a little whippersnapper, and Holden wouldn't have been able to argue. The child never failed to say something completely unexpected.

Deciding not to respond to Zack's comment, he continued, "While Jonah was on the ship, God sent a terrible storm. It was so bad the crew was afraid the ship would rip in two. Jonah knew the storm was his fault, so you know what he did?"

"Told them to throw him overboard," said Vince.

"Yep." Holden moved Jonah out of the boat.

Zack scrunched up his face. "That's the craziest thing I ever heard. Just 'cause I do something bad doesn't mean I'm gonna tell my mom to throw me out the window."

Holden said, "But the Bible tells us that Jonah did tell the sailors to throw him overboard. Do you know what happened after that?"

"God sent a great big fish to swallow Jonah," said Sean.

Holden placed a fish on the board and then put Jonah

on top of it. "That's right, and Jonah stayed in the belly of the fish for three days, praying to God."

"Then the fish spit Jonah onto the shore," said John.

Holden nodded, and Zack jumped up again. "Now wait a minute. Let's think about this." The boy scratched his head. "Jonah would have been covered in fish slime and guts and blood." His face brightened. "That is so cool." Then he scrunched up his nose and waved his hand in front of it. "Except the smell. Fish smell disgusting."

Trying to stay on track, Holden motioned for Zack to sit down again. "But you know what Jonah did? He obeyed God, and he went and told the Ninevites they needed to stop being bad and follow God's ways. And what do you think happened?"

"They did what Jonah said," replied Vince.

Holden switched the piece with angry people to one of a group of happy people. "So when Jonah stopped running from God, and did what he was supposed to do, a whole lot of people started following God."

"What does this story teach us?" asked Jake.

"That you better not get in a boat if you're gonna run from God, 'cause you don't want to get all covered in guts and smell like fish!" Zack declared.

"Or," Jake said with emphasis, "you should just do what God says to begin with."

The boy shrugged, as if that option would be all right, as well.

While Holden got their snack ready, Jake took out the box of puppets and the boys reenacted the story with each other. When class ended, Megan joined them in picking up the trash and putting the puppets away.

Watching his best friend interact with his fiancée and soon-to-be stepson, Holden realized he wanted that with Ava. Everyone around him seemed to be finding their spouses. Even his dad had fallen for someone. Holden wanted what they had, but just as Jonah ran from God, the woman he loved still ran from him.

Ava stood beside Clyde as he held the back of the chair and bent his knees. "Great job. Let's count to five."

"One, two, three, four, five," he muttered, before he straightened his legs. "You're killing me, Ava."

His words tugged at her heartstrings. She could tell he didn't feel well today, and not from the usual grumpiness. He'd been sick with bronchitis the last week and hadn't been able to move around as much as he needed to. As a result, his joints were stiffer than usual. "One more time."

He groaned.

"For me." She grabbed the other chair and placed it beside his. "I'll do it with you."

The corner of Clyde's mouth lifted just a bit as he nodded. They bent together, counted to five and then straightened their knees again.

She picked up his chart off the counter, then walked him back to the lobby. "Clyde, be sure to do your exercises this week. I know they're going to hurt, but you need to keep trying."

He growled as he waited for Katie to arrange his next appointment. "You young people think you can tell me what to do."

"You're right about that," the teen piped, before she handed him an appointment card. "And what would you do without us?"

He curled his lip, but not before Ava noted the quick glimmer of amusement in his eyes. She waved to him. "Take care, Clyde."

He grumbled as he and his wife walked out the door. Ava saw Holden and motioned for him to come on back.

"He seemed happy," said Holden.

"Don't let him fool you. He's a total sweetheart."

Holden sat in the chair, then took off his boots and socks. His ankle was no longer swollen or bruised, and he walked on it with ease. Even though he didn't need to keep coming, she knew he would for the full six weeks. And really, she didn't want to stop seeing him. She'd enjoyed getting to know him again.

During his last visit he'd told her about some of the dates he'd gone on since she'd left Surprise. Though the fact that he'd dumped a plate of spaghetti on a girl's lap was funny, Ava had still felt a niggling of jealousy. She'd been able to share the story of only one foiled date of her own when his body language had made it clear he didn't want to think about her dating other people. She liked that he was jealous.

"How does your ankle feel?" she asked.

"Still a little tender."

"Hmm." She lifted his foot and massaged around the joint. No swelling. No tension that she could feel. "Okay, go ahead and start with the alphabet."

While Holden completed his exercises, he told her about the crazy antics of the little redheaded boy who'd gone to lunch with them. The kid was quite a character, and Holden's feelings for the boy were evident, but she wished he'd talk about something else.

A knock sounded, then Rick opened the door. "Hope I'm not disturbing you." He nodded toward Holden.

Ava shook her head. "That's okay. Do you need me?"

He stepped inside the room, then pulled two baseball tickets out of his jacket pocket. "I have these Arizona Diamondbacks tickets for tomorrow night's game against the Chicago White Sox, and none of us are able to go. I wondered if you might want them."

Ava furrowed her brow. "That's really nice of you, but I don't watch baseball, and I'd hate for you not to give them to someone…"

Rick leaned against the counter. "You don't have to be a big fan of the game. Everyone should go at least once, just for the experience."

"Well, I…"

"I can even let you off an hour early." He flipped the tickets. "I just hate to see them go to waste."

Ava blinked. "I…I'm not sure who I would take. I guess…"

"I'll go with you." Holden grinned wider than the Cheshire cat from *Alice in Wonderland*. Then he pursed his lips. "I mean, I can if you need someone, at the last minute like this."

Ava narrowed her gaze. "Since when do *you* like baseball?"

Holden lifted his palms. "It's like your boss said. I can go just for the experience."

Ava took the tickets from Rick. "I guess it's settled. Thanks for thinking of me."

Her boss opened the door. "Just glad they're not going to waste."

They finished the session, then she guided Holden back to the lobby. "I guess I'll pick you up tomorrow after I get off work."

"You don't have to do that," he said. "I can drive. Just call me when you're ready."

She crossed her arms and cocked her head. "I'm kinda wondering if you set this up."

Holden lifted his hands. "That's the first time I've seen your boss. I promise."

"Okay." Ava chuckled at his pleading expression. "I'll see you tomorrow then."

He walked out the door. Once it closed, Katie burst out laughing beside her. Ava turned toward her young friend and gasped. "It was you. You set that up."

Katie smacked the arm of the chair. "It was miserable, watching the two of you make goo-goo eyes every time he came in, yet neither of you asked the other out."

Ava swatted her. "Katie!"

"Are you saying you don't want to go with him?"

Ava lifted her right shoulder. "I didn't say that."

Katie pointed at her. "See? You do want to go out with him. Just let the past go and move on. You two are adorable together."

Ava pulled the tickets out of her pocket and tapped them against her palm. She was putting the past behind her. Each session with Holden had proved more enjoyable than the one before.

Katie had taken her advice, and all had gone well for her and Corey. Ava would take Katie's advice in turn. Forget the past and move on.

Your past had an effect on Holden, and he doesn't even know it.

Ava pushed the thought away. She'd go out with him and have a terrific time. He wouldn't want to know everything, anyway.

Chapter 13

Holden took Ava's hand as he led her up the stairs to the seat numbers printed on the tickets. They sat behind third base, not terribly high up, and were able to see the oversize screen behind home plate with ease. He supposed they were good seats, though he'd never even watched a full baseball game on television, let alone viewed one in person.

Out of habit, he reached to pull down the brim of his cowboy hat against the sun, then remembered he'd put it away for the day. He was thankful for his sunglasses, but the hat would have offered additional shade from the hot Arizona sun.

People of all ages and sizes filled the seats around them. Some were decked out in red-and-black Diamondback attire, and were already overly excited from their choice of drink. The smells of popcorn and roasted peanuts filled the air, and he might have enjoyed the aroma if he didn't already feel as if he was on sensory overload from the sight and sounds of the crowd.

He glanced at Ava. She looked especially adorable in a white-and-red jersey, with her hair pulled back in a Diamondbacks cap. He pointed to the number. "Who's the player?"

She shrugged. "I don't know. It's Katie's. She told me to wear it."

Holden chuckled. "Would you like a drink or snack?"

"Maybe in a minute." She looked around. "Let's wait until everyone gets settled into their seats."

He had a feeling there wouldn't be much more settling. He enjoyed wide-open spaces with cattle grazing. A packed church was about as crowded as he preferred to be. Noting two heavyset men sporting cut-up red-and-black T-shirts and red painted faces, he couldn't deny he'd never been much of a sports guy.

People continued to file up and down the steps. Ava looked as overwhelmed as he felt, and with the never-ending noise around them, he decided to wait to try to talk with her.

A man walked onto the field with a microphone, and the crowd burst into wild applause and cheers. They stood when a young boy, who apparently performed well on some television competition, sang the national anthem. A couple teenage girls a few seats below them swooned and then squealed at ear-piercing decibels when the kid finished. If it was possible, the crowd seemed louder and more obnoxious when the guy announced that the game was about to start.

It was soon under way, and the fans screamed or booed as one player after another went up to bat. Holden tried to enjoy himself, and maybe the whole experience wouldn't have been so bad if he wasn't sitting so close to a guy who was every bit as big as him. His personal bubble, as his dad called it, was being invaded, and Holden didn't like it one bit.

A player walked out to home plate. The crowd burst into wild applause. Holden leaned toward Ava. "That's your guy?"

She frowned. "Huh?"

He pointed to her shirt. "You're wearing his number."

"Oh." She shifted in her seat. "I hope he's good."

The guy hit a home run, and everyone around them jumped to their feet, hollering and waving red-and-black hand towels. Holden gave her a thumbs-up, then mouthed, "I guess he is."

Once most of the people sat back down, Ava tapped his shoulder. "I'll be right back."

He shifted to allow her to get out, and watched as she walked down the stairs. When a teen walked by selling roasted peanuts, he bought a bag, then popped one in his mouth. Several minutes went by and Ava still hadn't come back. He hoped she hadn't forgotten where they were seated. He checked his phone, but hadn't received any texts from her.

After eating more peanuts, he ended up buying a large soft drink, as well. The inning ended and Ava still hadn't returned. Worried, he glanced at his phone again. No text. Deciding to check on her, he made his way down the stairs, then spotted her standing near the entrance. "Hey. You okay?"

She touched the bill of her cap. "I'm sorry, Holden. I don't want to ruin this for you, but I just couldn't take all the noise." She fanned her face. "And everyone was just so..."

"Close."

"Yes."

Holden smiled. "I was trying to hang in there for you. Baseball games are definitely not for me."

Ava grinned with obvious relief. "You mean it?"

"Definitely."

She exhaled. "I was trying so hard to be a good sport and not ruin it for you, but when the woman sitting beside me squealed that ear-piercing scream with the last home run..." Ava shook her head. "I just had to get some air."

"Why don't we head out of here and get something to eat?"

She tapped her hat. "A fancy restaurant is definitely out."

"You look really cute in that hat."

Ava huffed. "Please." She flipped the bottom of the jersey. "I feel like a boy."

"You definitely don't look like one."

Her cheeks bloomed pink, and Holden grabbed her elbow and guided her out of the stadium. "How about some pizza?"

"That sounds great." She puckered her lips. "What should I tell Rick about the game? I don't want to seem ungrateful, but I definitely don't want any more free tickets."

"Tell him you were able to experience a baseball game just as he said everyone should."

Once at the truck, he opened the door and helped her into the cab. She grinned at him. "You still like bacon and pineapple?"

"I never liked bacon and pineapple. That was your favorite."

She tapped her chin as a mischievous smile curved her lips. "Oh, that's right. I guess it still is."

He cocked his head. "Do you remember my favorite pizza toppings?"

She lifted her finger. "Meat, meat and more meat."

"Yep." He shut the door and walked around the truck.

Each moment he spent with Ava he felt more certain that his feelings for her had never gone away. He still loved her.

Ava licked the blueberry gelato from the spoon. "Aunt Irene, this was a great idea."

Her aunt pulled the straw out of her chocolate milkshake, scooped off a dollop of whipped cream and popped it into her mouth. "I know Rita's is your favorite, and I didn't know if you'd taken time to get some ice cream since moving back to Surprise."

Ava relished the cool, fruity goodness as she shook her head. "I can't believe I've been here more than two and a half months and hadn't stopped by."

Katie took a bite of her mint chocolate chip blendini with extra chocolate. "You'll never make that mistake again. I'm making you come here at least once a week."

Aunt Irene frowned as Phoebe stirred the straw in her Italian ice. "What's the matter? You don't like it?"

Her friend smacked her lips. "Must have been the pear flavor I liked so well. This key lime is too sour."

"You told her green," said Aunt Irene.

"I know. That's because I couldn't remember which flavor I like."

Ava swallowed a spoonful of her gelato, then swung her legs out of the booth. "I'll get you the one you like, Phoebe."

"No, no." She touched Ava's hand. "That's sweet of you, but I'm not going to waste a perfectly good Italian ice." She sucked on her straw, then puckered her lips before grinning. "Already starting to grow on me."

Aunt Irene dabbed her mouth with a napkin. "Did I tell you that the pattern for my outfit arrived?"

"The one for Senior Idol?" asked Katie.

She nodded.

"I've never been before, but Mom and Ava say you sing really well."

"You'll have to come this year with Ava." Aunt Irene touched her neck. "Phoebe and I found the perfect sewing pattern for a cowgirl dress, and I ordered some red-checkered material, and—"

Phoebe swatted Aunt Irene's arm. "Don't tell them what it looks like. It should be a surprise."

"Fine," she snapped, then grinned back at them. "Jerry and I are gonna look for a cowboy hat for him this weekend."

Phoebe rolled her eyes. "I never see my friend anymore, now that she has a boyfriend."

Aunt Irene nudged her. "Oh, stop it. We still see each other all the time."

Ava enjoyed spending time with her aunt and Phoebe. The two had been friends longer than Ava had been alive, and she doubted Aunt Irene's budding relationship with Jerry would change that. Though they teased mercilessly, their friendship was one to be admired.

Katie whispered, "Are they always like this?"

"Pretty much," Ava chuckled. "So, how are things with Corey?"

Her expression brightened. "He just got a call last week for an interview with the police department in Phoenix." She twirled her hands. "It's a long process, but at least the interview is a start."

"That's great," said Aunt Irene. "Corey must be your boyfriend."

The teen nodded.

"And how about you?" Phoebe pointed to Ava. "Any new beaus since moving to Surprise?"

She shook her head, and Katie gasped and pushed her with her shoulder. "What about Holden?"

Phoebe's eyebrows rose. "Holden Whitaker?"

"We're just friends." Ava twisted the napkin, knowing she'd already lost her heart to him again. He'd been seeing her for physical therapy for a month. Katie had tricked them into attending the Diamondbacks' game, and then somehow she'd ended up having a quick dinner with him a couple times. Each moment she spent with him she fell more head over heels.

"I'd say they're more than friends." Katie leaned forward. "Last week he brought in flowers for her." She lifted two fingers. "For the second time."

Ava bit her bottom lip. She'd forgotten about the flowers. The gestures had been sweet, and he'd gotten her favorites both times. He remembered so many things about her.

"And," Katie continued, "he showed up at the clinic a couple of days ago when she was getting off work, and insisted she go to dinner with him. Said he owed her something for all the help she'd given him with his ankle." Katie snorted. "None of the other clients take you out to eat. They just pay the bill."

Ava studied her aunt's face, trying to read her thoughts. She hadn't told her how much time she'd been spending with Holden. Not that Aunt Irene would mind; she loved him and would approve of him without question. And yet Ava still hesitated to talk to her about him.

"In fact," Katie went on, "he made her promise to let him take her out tomorrow night. Wouldn't tell her where they would be going, but she agreed."

Ava's jaw dropped. "How would you know that?"

Katie shrugged. "Thin walls."

"More like a big snoop."

"Maybe that, too." The teen twirled her straw. "But

just so you know, it was Mom who told me about that. She really likes Holden."

"He's a great guy," said Aunt Irene.

Phoebe shook her head. "Little terror as a boy." She blew out a breath, then looked at Irene. "Remember how we dreaded when he came into Sunday school?" She snapped her fingers. "Remember the time he snuck a baby frog in his pants pocket and scared the whole class half to death?"

Aunt Irene cackled. "I sure do."

Phoebe lifted her finger. "Terror as a boy, but he's certainly grown into a fine young man."

Katie started up again. "Yeah. I guess Ava and Holden had some kind of history together—" she pointed to Aunt Irene "—when she lived with you before. She was all worried about whatever happened then, but I told her you gotta let go of the past. We're living in the present."

Aunt Irene's voice was just above a whisper. "But you have to face your past before you can let it go."

Chapter 14

With two large lemonades in his hands, Holden walked to Ava and the blanket she'd spread out on the grass inside Surprise Stadium. She could have been mistaken for a model, sitting there with her face turned up to the sun. One hand rested on the blanket behind her back and the other draped over her slightly bent legs. She wore a pretty purple sundress for him. At least, he believed she wore it for him, as he'd always loved her in purple.

The Arizona heat of May still bore down on them, but the sun would be setting soon, and the temperature would drop as well. He offered her a cup. "Here you go."

"Thanks." She took a sip, then squinted and puckered her lips. "Really good, but really sour."

"First sip'll get you every time." He settled down beside her and gazed around at the families, with varying ages of children, spreading towels and blankets in preparation for the movie. For years, Surprise Stadium had been showing family-friendly movies during the summer months. Concessions were open, but the movie and the seats were free, though Holden preferred to lounge on a blanket on the grass. Many families shared his sentiment.

"This is my kind of ball game," Ava said.

The screens lit up with a commercial before the movie. She kicked off her sandals, then leaned back on her elbows. "Remember, this is how we used to do it."

Holden remembered. They'd come to a free movie almost eight years ago. She'd watched some full-length Disney cartoon, and he'd watched her. The same thing would happen tonight.

He'd thought he loved her then, and he had. As much as a twenty-year-old man could love a barely-out-of-high-school girl. He was committed to her, and if she hadn't run off to college, they'd have worked through their relationship the hard way.

Now his feelings plunged to a deeper level. Though he saw snippets of the teenage Ava, when she teased about pizza and then flopped back on the blanket to watch the movie, he appreciated the grown-up Ava more. The woman who guided patients through physical therapy with confidence and kindness, who cared for her aunt and family.

The movie started, and Ava laughed at one of the characters' antics. Holden tried to focus on the show, but the truth was he didn't like to watch movies. He grew bored easily, and soon found himself watching Ava, or the couple beside them with a small girl and baby. He and Ava could marry and start a family. She was out of college. He was established with his dad on the ranch. He loved Ava. She was the only woman he'd ever envisioned having a future with.

The movie ended, and they headed to the truck. Before

starting the engine, he said, "I thought we'd take a walk on the trail."

She looked surprised, but said, "Okay."

The trail had been their spot, the place they'd told each other "I love you." Where they'd had their first kiss, and where he'd told her he wanted to marry her.

He pulled into White Tank Mountains Regional Park and stopped the truck. After going around and opening the door for her, he took her hand in his. She didn't pull away.

"The park won't be open much longer," Ava whispered.

He looked at the time on his smartphone. "We still have an hour."

He expected her to let go, but she didn't. His heart pounded as his mind raced, trying to figure out the words he wanted to say. *I want you to be my girlfriend.* They just seemed too old for that. *I still love you.* Those words would probably scare her off. *Will you date me? I care about you. I've never gotten over you.* The more he debated, the more confused and uncertain he became.

Ava stopped, jolting Holden from his thoughts. A cactus towered twenty feet or more above them. The mountains rose in the background. "Remember this?"

Of course he did. He'd been so busy worrying about what to say that he'd almost walked past the place he'd spent more than one night dreaming about. "Vividly."

He gazed down at her. When she looked into his eyes, he saw the Ava who had loved him with all her being. He cupped her chin with his hand, finding her skin as soft as he remembered. Bending down, he pressed his lips to hers.

For a moment, he thought she wouldn't return the kiss, but then she trailed her arms around his neck and pulled him closer. He was dreaming. Surely, this wasn't really happening.

When she broke away, Holden was breathless. He

couldn't remember the walk back to the truck or the drive to her aunt's house. When he walked Ava to the door, he kissed her again. This time she touched his cheek and gazed into his eyes before saying goodnight.

Everything in the world seemed right as, a short time later, he rushed into his bedroom and rummaged through the bottom dresser drawer. When he couldn't find the item fast enough, he threw every pair of shorts he owned onto the floor. Finding the black box, he gently took it out of the drawer, then plopped onto the bed.

He took a deep breath before he opened the box for the first time in eight years. The purchase had been made before Ava left. Popping the top, he stared at the single marquise-cut diamond and white-gold band. Though the ring was simple, the diamond was good-sized, a full carat. He'd sold his old work truck to buy it for her.

Grinning, he took the ring out of the box. He'd been foolish back then. If she'd stayed and agreed to marry him, he would have needed that truck on the ranch. *Her running the way she did was probably a good thing. We weren't ready.*

He replaced the ring in the box and tucked it back into the drawer. *But we are now.*

Ava floated into the house, her heart still beating quickly. She waved to her aunt as she made her way into the bathroom and shut the door. Gripping the sides of the sink, she leaned forward and stared at her reflection. "That was wonderful," she whispered.

Still gazing at her reflection, she bit her bottom lip, then slowly lifted her hand and pressed her fingertips against her mouth. Her heart pounded as she thought of Holden's lips pressed against hers. She'd forgotten how much she loved to kiss him.

Tingles shot through her as her mind and heart conjured all the memories with Holden. Her first love. *My only love.*

She wrapped her fingers tighter around the pedestal sink and dipped her head. *God, how can I feel so much love for him?* She made a fist and pressed it against her chest. *My heart actually hurts.*

Tears filled her eyes, then rolled down her cheeks. Undressing, she started the shower, as hot as she could stand it. The water rained against her skin and she wet her hair.

Love was tidy. It was calculated. Superficial. All surface. Love was financial provisions. Food. Shelter. Clothes. A good education.

But not here. Not in Surprise, Arizona. She loved God. He was her Lord and Savior, but in this city, He was also her friend and daily guide. Here, she had an aunt who pampered her and talked to her, who wanted to know how her day had gone and how she was feeling.

And Holden was here. A shiver rushed through Ava, and she turned down the cold to make the water hotter. She'd never loved a person with every ounce of her being as she had Holden. Which was the reason she'd run away. The feeling was too strong. Too scary. Too all-encompassing.

She closed her eyes. *That's not true.* There was someone else she'd loved as much as Holden.

Her feet, which had felt as if they were floating only minutes before, became heavy concrete blocks, weighing her down. Keeping her immobile. She turned off the shower, dried herself, then slipped into her robe. She couldn't see her reflection in the fogged up mirror. She didn't want to.

Running the comb through her hair, she plodded to her bedroom. Aunt Irene sat on the corner of the bed. She folded her hands in her lap. "We need to talk."

Ava wasn't surprised. She wouldn't even argue. Lowering herself into the wingback chair beside the desk, she said, "I'm listening."

Aunt Irene opened her mouth, then shut it and pursed her lips. The heaviness in Ava's heart increased, and somehow her mind had gone blank. She wondered how she could go from such deep, vivid feelings of love and happiness to complete and utter emptiness.

"Until Katie mentioned it the other day, I didn't realize you and Holden were seeing each other again. I guess I've been preoccupied with my own life. I hope I haven't neglected you."

Ava looked at her aunt. "You have never neglected me. I've never told you how much your support has meant. All my life you've been my constant. Especially when I needed you most."

Aunt Irene walked to her and kissed the top of her head. "You're special, Ava. God has always had a plan for you. Do you believe that?"

She sighed. "In my head, yes. When I'm in His Word, yes. When bad things happen, it's hard."

Aunt Irene sat back on the bed. Ava didn't look at her, but she could feel her aunt watching. She envisioned her lips moving as she prayed for peace over Ava. She had heard and felt her aunt do it before, years ago, when Ava had thought she'd die from the pain.

"Have you told him?" Aunt Irene's voice was just above a whisper. The words seemed to brush Ava's cheek like a kiss of death.

She shook her head. A flood of despair filled the emptiness in her heart and mind. She heard Job's words from scripture as an audible voice in her mind: *If I am guilty— woe to me!*

She *was* guilty. "I was punished." The words slipped out.

Aunt Irene took her hand and guided her to the bed beside her. She wrapped her arms around Ava and pressed her face against her shoulder. "My sweet child, you were not punished. There are things we will never understand this side of heaven. That is one of them."

Bitter sobs escaped Ava's lips as she clung to the only woman who'd shown her physical affection. "I don't want to tell him. I don't even want to say the words."

Her aunt rocked back and forth and patted her head. "I know. I know." Then she whispered, "But you must."

Ava closed her eyes and let misery consume her. Her aunt continued to rock and hum. Soon, she sang an old hymn Ava hadn't heard in a long time. The beginning was a jumble in Ava's mind, then she heard, "'When sorrows like sea billows roll, whatever my lot, Thou hast taught me to say, it is well, it is well with my soul.'"

Ava sniffed as she held her aunt tightly. Her soul was not well.

Chapter 15

The last week had been exceptionally busy, with several cows giving birth. Two of them had to have some help, so Holden had gotten little sleep and even less time to talk to Ava. They'd texted a few times, but she seemed to have had a busy week, as well.

But the week was behind them and at any moment both their families would join him and Dad for a Memorial Day lunch.

"Son, get the hamburgers and hot dogs out of the refrigerator for me," Jerry called from the back deck. "I'm going to go ahead and get 'em started."

Holden grabbed the meat and took it out to him, then set the condiments on the counter. The front door opened and Sara, Daryl, Traci and Carl all walked inside together. Daryl set Sara's homemade coleslaw on the table, and Carl placed a tray of brownies smothered in hot fudge icing beside it.

"Mmm, I smell the grill," said Traci.

Sara giggled. "I'm surprised Irene's letting Dad eat red meat."

"It's good he's eating better. His blood pressure's been down a bit," responded Holden.

Sara reached up and pinched his cheek. "Don't go getting all defensive, little brother. I'm glad she's keeping an eye on him."

"I just can't believe he's listening," said Traci.

Sara nodded. "My point exactly."

Holden looked over her head and out the door. He was surprised Ava and Irene hadn't yet arrived.

Sara punched his stomach, and he let out a grunt. "Don't worry. Your girlfriend will be here soon enough."

Holden flicked her arm. "You're lucky you're old and married, or I'd throw you on the floor and beat you up."

Traci snorted. "I'd help her, and the two of us would whip you."

Ava's car pulled in the driveway just then and the family got out. His heart pounded at how beautiful and patriotic Ava looked in a blue jean sundress with a red necklace and belt.

She smiled, then averted her gaze as she walked into the house. Probably a bit bashful after the last two kisses they'd shared. If she was half as affected as he'd been, she'd thought of them often the last week.

Dad walked into the great room with a plateful of grilled hamburgers and hot dogs. He lifted his free hand in the air. "All right, we're all here. I'm ready to eat."

Irene kissed his cheek, then hustled Mitch and Matt into the kitchen with the dishes she'd brought. The families formed a line and filled their plates. Though hungry, Holden took no more than a spoonful of everything. He had plans to take Ava for a walk after lunch, and he didn't want to be stuffed and uncomfortable.

Just as they had almost two months ago, the families paired off into couples around the table, leaving Holden between Matt and Ava. This time he didn't mind sitting beside her.

"I like your dress. You look pretty," he said.

"Thanks." She took a small bite of a deviled egg.

Matt leaned forward and pointed in front of Holden. "Did you end up putting paprika on the eggs? You know I hate paprika."

"No, I didn't," Ava snapped.

Holden lifted his brows. They must have been squabbling a bit before coming over. He understood. When the girls were still at home the whole family had ended up in huge battles anytime they went anywhere together.

She was quiet, and Holden decided not to start any conversations until lunch was over and they could spend time alone. Irene looked at them so often he wondered if he had food on his face.

He wiped his mouth with the napkin before taking another bite of his hamburger. Each couple was engrossed in their own conversations. Mitch and Ellie seemed to be getting more serious. They were such an odd pair, but Holden was glad Mitch had such a positive person in his life.

Traci cleared her throat and tapped her glass with a fork. "Dad, I have a present for you." She elbowed Carl, and he disappeared into the kitchen, then returned with a small wrapped box.

Dad frowned. "A present. Why? It's not my birthday. I wasn't in the military."

Traci grinned. "I know, but when I saw them I just knew you had to have 'em." She took the box from Carl and gave it to Dad.

Irene pushed his arm. "Well, go ahead and open it. We can't wait to see."

Dad unwrapped the present and lifted the lid. He pulled out a pair of earplugs. His lip curled up in a smile. "Thank you."

Traci clapped her hands, then bent forward, laughing. "Now, read what's at the bottom of the box."

Dad scrunched his nose. "What is that?"

Irene peeked inside, then gasped. She covered her mouth with her fingers.

Carl laughed out loud. "Read it, Jerry."

"It says you'll need these in November."

Holden smiled as he realized what Traci and Carl were trying to tell his dad.

Irene pointed inside again. "Jerry, that's an ultrasound picture of your grandson or granddaughter."

Dad's mouth fell open as everyone broke out into cheers. Sara hopped up and wrapped Traci in a big hug, and Holden hugged them both.

Their dad wiped his eyes with a napkin and said, "A grandbaby." He stood and kissed Traci on the cheek, then patted Carl's back. "I'm so happy for you both."

Ava dabbed her own eyes before she congratulated them. Irene gave her a quick hug, then Ava left in the direction of the bathroom.

Holden wasn't sure if she didn't feel well or if she was just excited for his sister. He remembered how his sisters used to cry if the other one did. Sara and Traci both wiped their eyes with the back of their hands now, proving his memory true.

When Ava came out of the bathroom, she walked to him and placed her hand on his arm. "Holden, do you mind if we take a walk?"

His heart flipped in his chest. He lifted his index finger. "Just one moment."

He raced into his bedroom, pulled the black box out

of the drawer, then dropped it in his front pocket. Today would be a day he'd never forget.

Ava tried to keep her emotions at bay as she waited for Holden. What were the chances of Traci and Carl sharing such exciting news today of all days? She was happy for them, or at least she genuinely wanted to be. *God, these are the times when I feel like I'm being punished. I know I was wrong, and I deserve punishment.*

Scripture she'd read time and again flowed through her mind. *You, Lord, are forgiving and good, abounding in love to all who call you.*

Holden walked back down the hall and took her hand in his. She held it tightly, needing to memorize the coarseness of his skin and the strength of his grip. In all the commotion, no one noticed they were leaving except Aunt Irene, who nodded and mouthed, "I'm praying."

Her aunt had comforted her several times in the last week, and in a way, Ava's wounded spirit had healed more in the last seven days than in the last seven years. But today promised to be one she would never forget.

They walked outside and past the barn. Creosote bushes dotted the dry ground all around them as they headed toward one of the ponds on the ranch.

"I'm sorry we haven't had a chance to talk this week." She needed to start with something light to build her courage.

Holden lowered his cowboy hat against the sun. "I can't remember when I've been so busy." He squeezed her hand. "It was like we had a really great time together and then the ranch went nuts. I bet I was up thirty or more hours straight, helping calves make an entrance into the world."

"We were busy at the clinic. Got three new patients last

week, and I helped Aunt Irene and the decorating committee fix up the sanctuary for church yesterday."

Holden touched his front pocket, then swiped his hand against his jeans. "Y'all did—" his voice caught, and he cleared his throat "—a good job. I always enjoy the church's tribute to our veterans for Memorial Day weekend."

"I don't think I'll ever fully be able to comprehend how much I am thankful for our military." Though she was stalling, Ava meant every word. A sense of pride stirred in her chest each time she saw a man or woman in uniform. She admired their courage, strength, and willingness to put America's best interests before their own lives.

They reached the pond and Holden stopped walking. He turned toward her and took both her hands in his. She looked past him at the White Tank Mountains rising in the distance. She'd visited their trail many times since moving back to Surprise. God surrounded her with His peace and calm in that place. There, she poured out her heart to Him, and He soaked up her fear and pain and loved her anyway.

Holden rubbed his thumbs against the top of her hands. She gazed into his blue eyes and knew she'd never love another man the way she loved Holden. He'd torn down the walls that had boarded up her heart when she was just a teenage girl, and she'd never been able to fully mend them.

"Ava, I have enjoyed every moment with you the last six weeks." He kicked his right boot against the left. "You've fixed me up, and now I won't be able to see you at the clinic anymore."

She bit her bottom lip as the finality of their time together pressed upon her. "I know. I'll miss you."

A slow grin curved his lips. "For eight years I have missed you. I didn't realize just how much until you came back." His thumbs pressed against her skin with more fervency. Vulnerability filled his gaze, and he swallowed. "I still love you, Ava. I never stopped."

She wanted to tell him she loved him, too. How her heart soared and broke at the same time, hearing those words from him. Knowing he loved her, but in a matter of moments would loathe her. "Holden, I need to—"

He pulled a black box out of his front shirt pocket and dropped to one knee. Ava gasped and pressed her fingers against her lips. No. He wasn't doing this.

Holding the closed box in one hand, he gazed up at her. "I bought this ring eight years ago. Sold my old brown work truck to buy it."

Ava blinked. "What? You did what?"

Holden nodded. "Yes, Ava. I called, and when you wouldn't answer or respond to my messages, I bought this ring and drove to the college. When you still wouldn't see me, I debated on trying to get my money back. But I just couldn't do it." He opened the box. "I think it's because one day I'd be giving it to you."

Ava stared at the large marquise-cut diamond set on a white-gold band. Simple, but absolutely beautiful.

"Will you marry me?"

Reality crashed down on her when she heard those words, then looked into his eyes. Tears welled up and rolled down her cheeks. "Oh, Holden."

She yanked her hands away from him and rushed back to the house. Despite questions from their families, she grabbed her purse off the counter and raced out the door. Jumping in the car, she started the engine. She had to run.

Chapter 16

Still kneeling on one knee, Holden dipped his head. *God, what was I thinking? I always move too fast.* He looked up and watched her race in the back door of the house. Glancing up at the sky, he prayed, "God, what do I do?"

The heavens were quiet. The last time he'd chased after her she'd refused to see or speak to him, and eight years had passed. He pounded the ground with his fist. Not this time. He loved her, and he was tired of playing games. When a man knew what he wanted, he went for it. The same held true for a woman, and he knew Ava loved him. She was just too scared and stubborn to admit her feelings.

He marched back to the house and flung open the back door. Scanning the room, he ignored the surprised expressions of their families. "Where is she?" he demanded.

Irene walked from the front foyer, her hand cupped over her mouth. A tear slipped down her cheek. "Don't be angry. She knows she should have told you. Forgive her."

Dad stood and wrapped his arm around Irene. "Why are you crying, hon?" His attention turned to Holden. "And why did Ava just go running out that front door, wailing like a scolded toddler?"

"Holden!" Irene's voice squeaked. "She's beat herself up for so long."

Holden touched the woman's arm and leaned closer to her. "What are you talking about?"

His dad blustered, "I've raised you better than to make a girl cry like that. What did you say to Ava?"

"I asked her to marry me." Holden's voice boomed through the room. He looked around and saw expressions of pity on everyone's face. Embarrassment swelled within him, heating his cheeks and igniting his pride.

"She didn't tell you, did she?" Irene whispered as she shook her head.

Holden smacked his thigh, then raked his fingers through his hair. "Didn't tell me what? Irene, what are you talking about?"

She took his elbow and led him to the front door. "You have to go."

"I'm not going anywhere." He pointed to the floor. "I'm standing right here until you tell me whatever it is that's eating Ava."

Her aunt shook her head again and waved her hand. "No. Just go. Right now."

He spread his fingers. "Go where? Where am I supposed to go?"

Her hands trembled, and Jerry took them in his. "Irene, hon, what is it?"

She snapped her fingers. "My house. She'll have to go home first. She's a mess. Won't be able to go anywhere public." Irene hugged Holden, then kissed his forehead. "Don't leave until she tells you."

He hopped into the truck and took off. Ava had been keeping something from him, but what? She had a boyfriend? She was married? He growled. *She better not be married.* Maybe she'd gotten divorced. What could possibly be so bad she kept running away from him at every turn? *How hard is it to just be honest?*

Anger and frustration swirled in his mind and heart. He pounded his fist against the steering wheel. Pity. His family and hers felt sorry for him. Poor Holden, so in love, but not loved back.

And his dad getting mad at him. Acting as if Holden had done something wrong to make Ava and Irene cry. He pounded the steering wheel again. *God, I just love the woman. Want to make her my wife. What's so mean about that?*

He pulled into the driveway behind Ava's car. Relief that she was there washed over him, then hesitancy. The front door was slightly ajar, so he walked in. "Ava?"

No answer. Sobs sounded from down the hall. He followed the noise, then knocked on the bathroom door. "Ava?"

She gasped, and he heard a thump and a rattling of some kind. "Holden, what are you doing here? How did you get in the house?"

"The door was open." He swallowed the knot in his throat, feeling suddenly anxious. "We need to talk."

She sniffed. "Give me a minute."

Holden stepped back into the living room. Frustrated, he plopped onto the couch and dropped his elbow on the armrest. His arm caught the edge of a Bible and it fell to the floor. With a growl, he bent down. The front cover was open, and he saw his name written on the first page.

"What in the world?" he mumbled as he picked it up. His name was written under the subheading of Deaths. Beside it was a date in April, seven years ago.

"I should have told you."

Holden looked up. Ava stood a few feet away from him. Her face was red and splotchy, her eyes swollen from crying.

He frowned and pointed to the page. "I don't understand."

Ava's lower lip quivered as she crossed her arms in front of her and rubbed her biceps. "I…" She covered her face with her hands, then brought them down and pressed them against her chest. "We had a baby."

Holden looked back at the Bible. He thought of that night eight years ago. One night when their emotions had gotten away from them. He'd begged God's forgiveness, tried to apologize to Ava. He'd loved her and wanted to marry her.

He counted the months from that night to the date in the Bible. Eight months. Babies took nine, right? So the April date didn't make sense. But this child's name was written under Deaths. A child whose name was Holden.

Pain gripped his heart with such intensity his stomach churned and bile rose in his throat. He peered back up at Ava and knew the truth. "I had a son."

"Yes."

Ava sat in the chair across from Holden. She couldn't decipher his expression. Surprise. Hurt. Sadness. Anger. Glimmers of each emotion left their imprint in his eyes. He didn't move. His fingertip stayed pressed against their son's name in her Bible.

She rubbed her trembling hands together and took deep breaths, begging God to give her the right words to say. *Just be honest.*

Honesty, when it came to Holden, brought fear. When she was with him, she felt too much, loved too deeply.

Vulnerability wrapped around her like a blanket riddled with holes and lacking any warmth or comfort. She avoided pain and loss, and love brought the possibility of both.

Still, baby Holden had been his son. He had a right to know the truth. She rubbed her hands against her bare arms. "After that last night together…"

Holden stared at her with such intensity she wanted to crumble. She exhaled and started again. "After that night, I ran home. I was scared."

She couldn't share how deeply she'd felt for him, how that night had confirmed how desperately she loved him. So much that she'd given up her values and beliefs. But that wasn't love; it was infatuation. In her head, she knew that, and she'd run.

"I wanted to go to college. I wasn't ready to settle down as a wife."

She remembered how she'd mourned for Holden those first months of school. Determined to make her parents proud, she'd thrown herself into her schoolwork. She'd spent almost entire nights poring over papers and texts. Though she lived in the dorm where many of her peers were partying, she hadn't made one friend that first year. She barely spoke to her roommate.

Holden still stared at her, unmoving and expressionless. She clasped her hands again. "I didn't know I was pregnant until January. I've never been regular. I knew I'd gained some weight, but I thought that was normal. Freshman fifteen and all."

She tried to smile, but her lips dropped when she thought of the disbelief she'd felt when she'd purchased the pregnancy test. No one was with her when the test read positive. No one was there to tell her everything would be all right. She'd never before known such complete alone-ness and utter despair.

"I didn't believe the test could be true, so I didn't go to the doctor. I mean, we were together only one time." She paused, leaned her head back and blinked several times. "I finally went to the doctor in April. Everything seemed fine, but they scheduled an ultrasound to determine the due date and make sure everything was okay."

Her hands started to shake again, and she wrapped them around her waist. How she wished Holden would stop star-ing at her. Looking away, she felt more tears slip down her cheeks. She yanked a tissue from the box on the end table and wiped her eyes. "The ultrasound showed the baby was missing part of his brain. Within a week, I went into labor, and he was…he was dead."

She jumped from the chair and stared out the window. With the truth revealed, the heaviness in her chest light-ened. She turned and looked at Holden, then ached at the weight that now rested on him. Taking her keys off the counter, she said, "May I take you to his grave?"

Holden furrowed his brows into a straight line. "He's buried here?"

She nodded. Holden followed her to the car. He didn't speak as she drove, and she was glad for the reprieve. Glad not to have to explain more. She never went to the cemetery. Ever.

Her heart raced as she maneuvered the winding road inside the cemetery. Once parked a few yards from her family's purchased plots, she gripped the steering wheel and closed her eyes, praying God would give her strength.

Holden had already stepped out of her car and made his way toward her grandparents' markers. She wondered how she knew exactly where to walk, then remembered he'd gone with her and Aunt Irene to decorate the graves for Memorial Day then the Fourth of July all those years ago.

He stopped, and she knew he stood above their son's marker. Her legs wouldn't move, and she feared her heart would pound out of her chest. She never came here. Didn't want to see the place where her baby was buried.

God, help me.

Holden slumped as he covered his face with his hand. Then he took off his cowboy hat and laid it at the base of the marker. Empathy pushed her to him. She knew the heartache that stabbed deep into the core of his soul. Wrapping her arm around his shoulder, she whispered, "I'm so sorry."

He shrugged away and turned his face toward her. His eyes glazed with anger and tears. "Why didn't you tell me?"

"I should have."

He punched his finger against his chest. "How could you keep something like this from me?"

New tears streamed down her cheeks. "I don't know. I was scared."

He frowned. "Scared of what? Me?"

He stood and walked in a circle, raking his fingers through his hair, then clasping his hands behind his neck. "I didn't know. I would have done something. I could have helped."

Ava pressed her palms against her belly. "The doctor said it wasn't my fault, that there was nothing I could have done to change him." She shook her head. "But I know I should have gone to the doctor earlier."

Holden's face lit with challenge and fury. "Would that have made a difference? Would that have saved our son?"

Ava accepted the anger as added links to the chain of guilt she carried. She deserved the blame. "He said it wouldn't." She spread open her arms. "But I don't know."

Her gaze fell on the marker. She read the single letter,. *H.* She hadn't had his name etched out because she'd planned to never trouble Holden with the truth. Beside the letter was his date of birth and death. The same day. Falling to her knees, she leaned forward, pressing her fists against the ground and her face against her fists. For the thousandth time, she cried for forgiveness from God, from Holden, from her baby. She sobbed until her chest burned and her sides ached.

When she sat up, Holden was already in the car. They didn't speak as she drove back to her aunt's house. When she parked the car, she turned to him. "Holden, I am so sorry."

He got out, then looked in the open door. "He was my son, too, Ava."

Chapter 17

Holden and Jake sat at a shaded picnic table watching Vince and Zack play at the public pool. Holden had never been a recreational swimming kind of guy, but the kids had begged them after class, and here they were, sitting poolside sipping ice water. He glanced at Jake's ring finger. "I still can't believe you and Megan just up and got married."

"It shouldn't have been too big a surprise. I told you we were going to."

"But you just started dating—" Holden counted from March to June in his head "—three months ago."

Jake pointed to the boys as they slid down the water slides. "I knew going into the relationship how strongly I felt for Megan, and we didn't want to play around on account of Vince. He needs a father."

"Yeah, but you could've dated a little longer. I bet your mom had a fit."

"Nah. We told her we were heading to the courthouse.

She's been so wrapped in Jess's wedding she didn't seem to mind."

Holden leaned forward. "What did Jess say?"

Jake grinned. "I reckon she wasn't too happy that Megan and I beat her to the altar, so to speak."

Holden let out a howl. He figured Jake was putting her reaction lightly. Jess threw huge tantrums when things didn't go her way, and even though she was five years younger, she'd probably had a conniption fit that Jake married first.

Holden smacked the table. "Well, how is married life?"

"Wonderful."

"All you thought it'd be, huh?"

"Better."

Holden scrunched his nose. "Even the nagging and complaining?"

Jake clicked his tongue. "Ain't got there yet, though I suspect there'll be ups and downs."

"I'd say you're right." Holden wiped his forehead with the edge of a towel, then looked for the boys. He spied Zack's red hair. They stood in line at the slides again. Remembering that Zack's mom had said to put lotion on him a couple times, he looked at his smartphone. Next break he'd need to lather the kid up again.

"What happened with Ava?"

Holden frowned at his friend. "What do you mean?"

"I mean you've been crazy about her for months, years really. The two of you were talking, doing things together. Now, nothing."

Holden shrugged. "We were never really dating."

"So, you didn't care about her?"

"I didn't say that." His chest tightened as anger and sadness and longing mixed together within him. He didn't know a person could feel so many things at once. And his son. He'd never gotten to see or hold him. Hadn't even known he existed.

He'd be the same age as Zack. Almost exactly. He looked at the red-haired boy who challenged him every week. He'd teased that his son would be like Zack. Holden's heart ached anew at the thought.

Jake's voice lowered. "I'm sorry, man, if she didn't want to date."

"No. That's not what happened." He had no idea if she wanted to see him or not. Two weeks had passed since he'd found out about his son. He hadn't talked to her and didn't plan on it, either.

"What happened?"

He'd never told anyone about that night. They'd sinned, and he'd asked for forgiveness, but he'd also fallen completely in love with Ava. Wanted her to be his bride. And he would've never dreamed of saying anything against the woman he adored so deeply.

He still didn't want to hurt Ava, but the ache is his chest hurt sometimes to the point he thought he might die. He needed to talk to someone, and he was angry with God. Mad that He'd let Ava keep such a secret. Mad that He'd let Holden's son die. Noting Jake's sincere expression, Hol—den's resolve broke and he told his friend everything. About the night. Her running and him trying to talk to her. About asking her to marry him. About the baby.

Jake didn't say a word, but Holden saw the sadness in his friend's face. When he had spilled all his pain onto the wooden table, Jake grabbed his arm. "We're gonna pray."

Holden pulled it back. "No, we're not." He waved his hand. "First, we're at a pool. And second..." he hesitated "...I don't wanna."

Jake smacked his hand on top of Holden's. "Well, you're

going to, anyway. All you have to do is sit there. I'll do the praying."

Jake bowed his head, and Holden stared at the boys as they played on the water slides. Jake prayed that God would heal Holden's heart, and that he would forgive Ava and trust God with His sovereign will.

Holden swallowed back the knot in his throat. How could God's will be for his son to form without part of his brain? How was that sovereign?

Jake continued, "And God, I pray for Ava. How she must have hurt all these years, having not told Holden about their son."

Holden pursed his lips. How could Jake feel sorry for her?

"How alone she must have felt, keeping this all to herself. The guilt must have been unbearable."

Holden cleared his throat. He'd felt such guilt over the night, but that was the only pain he'd dealt with. He hadn't carried the baby, discovered the child would die, given birth to him, buried him. His heart twisted as he thought of Irene's words when she'd thought Holden already knew the truth. *Forgive her. She's beat herself up for so long.*

Anger slipped in and took control of his thoughts. If she'd told him, he would have helped her. They could have comforted each other. But she'd chosen to run away and keep secrets.

Looking at her reflection in the restroom mirror at the physical therapy clinic, Ava raked her fingers through her hair, then tried to fluff the top. She took a tube of lip gloss from her purse and applied the light pink color to her lips. She still looked tired.

Closing her eyes, she prayed for the millionth time that Holden would forgive her. With the truth exposed, she'd had time to think about her feelings for him. They were simple. She loved him.

God knew her heart, how she feared love, how guilt led her life. The Lord had spent the last two weeks wooing and loving her. She'd inhaled scripture like clean air and devoured prayer like a starving child. And God had wrapped her in His arms like a newborn baby. She simply couldn't get enough of Him. And for the first time she felt His forgiveness. More than just head knowledge, she knew heart knowledge, as well.

Despite the comfort she received from the Lord, she struggled to sleep, knowing Holden might not forgive her. Seeing him again on his knee with that little black box was her fervent prayer.

She joined Mary, Rick and Katie in the workroom for lunch. Mary pointed to the counter. "Save whatever you brought for lunch for tomorrow. We brought leftover tacos from last night."

Ava looked at the multiple containers of crunchy and soft taco shells, meat, refried beans, shredded cheese, lettuce, diced tomatoes, salsa and sour cream. "This looks delicious. When did you have time to set it all out?"

Katie raised her hand. "That was me." She took a bite of her taco, then lifted her chin and shoved a dangling piece of lettuce into her mouth.

Ava filled a plate, then sat at the table. Rick bit into his taco, then swallowed a drink of lemon water. "We have two added appointments today. Mary has to leave to take the boys to practice. I'll cover one. Will you be able to stay a little later and cover the other?"

"No problem."

Mary wiped her mouth. "The appointment will be after Clyde. We try to schedule him last because he seems to like to linger with you." She winked.

Rick smacked the table. "The man still won't see me, but he seems to really like the new girl."

Ava chuckled.

"Anyway," Mary said, "this appointment will be after Clyde. She's a girl from the high school. Gymnastics accident, if I remember correctly."

Ava swallowed a bite. "Like I said, no problem."

Katie dropped her taco to the table and leaned forward. "Ava, I forgot to tell you this morning."

"What?"

"Corey got a job." She clapped her hands. "He's going to be a Phoenix police officer."

"That's terrific."

Rick straightened. "We're really happy for him."

"Yep," said Mary. "He's a great kid."

"Which reminds me." Katie grinned. "How are things going with Holden?"

Ava sucked in a breath, causing part of the bite she'd just taken to go down the wrong way. She choked and coughed, tears welling in her eyes, while Rick pounded her back until she could finally breathe again. She lifted her finger and took several drinks of water.

"Sorry, Ava," Katie said. "Didn't mean to get you all choked up." She nudged her mom's elbow and giggled.

Ava rolled her eyes and dabbed them with a napkin. If she broke down in tears, she could blame them on her choking fit. "I haven't seen him in a couple weeks."

"What?" Mary and Rick said together.

"I thought you really liked each other," said Katie. "I mean, he looks at you like a kid looks at candy."

Ava shrugged. "Never know, I guess."

She stood and threw away the paper plate, hoping they wouldn't ask any more questions.

"Looks like it's time to get back to work," said Rick.

Ava turned and realized all three of them were staring at her with concerned expressions. She forced a full smile. "Yep. Busy afternoon ahead of us."

She tried not to think of Holden as she worked with her first and then second client after lunch, but each time she bumped into Rick or Mary they gave her the come-let-Mommy-and-Daddy-make-it-better faces. Katie was even less tactful. Each time Ava walked to the front to pick up a client, Katie would whisper, "I want all details after work today."

Ava wasn't sure she would be able to hold back the tears when the time came to pick up Clyde from the lobby. To her surprise, he carried a bouquet of wildflowers, including purple lupines and yellow poppies. He grinned as he handed them to her. "The wife and I noticed you've been a little down lately. Thought we'd pick you up some of those flowers your boyfriend got you."

"Clyde." She wrapped the old man in a hug. He patted her back, and a single tear slipped down her cheek. She sucked in her breath to keep any more at bay. She released him and smelled the flowers. "Thank you so much."

He motioned for her to head back to the room. "You're welcome, but my arthritis is acting up, and we need to get to work."

Once they arrived, he pointed to the door. "Go on. Run to the bathroom. Cry it out for a minute. I'm not going anywhere."

Tears filled her eyes as she tapped his knee. "You're really a sweet, sensitive guy at heart."

He huffed. "Well, don't go telling anybody." He shooed her away. "Just get on outta here."

Ava made her way to the restroom and splashed her face at the sink. Clyde had brought her flowers. She almost laughed out loud. She'd always known that deep down he was a sweetie. Whether Clyde knew it or not, God had used him to give her another one of His hugs. *Always provide right when I need it, don't you, Lord. The last eight years would have gone a lot smoother if I'd truly believed that to begin with.*

Chapter 18

Ava woke up the morning of the Fourth of July to find the sun shining through her window. The day promised to be a scorcher, and yet Aunt Irene had a packed schedule of plans. Practice for Senior Idol with Jerry in the morning. Clean and then fix a smorgasbord of food for dinner with his and her families. Then fireworks at Surprise Stadium in the evening.

The day before, Aunt Irene had fretted over not having time to decorate the grave markers of her parents for the Independence Day holiday. Ava's grandfather had been a veteran who'd fought in World War II. He loved the Fourth of July more than any other holiday, and Aunt Irene always made sure his grave reflected that passion. Not wanting her aunt to worry, Ava had offered to decorate.

Aunt Irene had been hesitant, then suggested the visit might do Ava some good. Walking into the living area, Ava stared now at the flowers and flags sitting on the floor, waiting for her to take them to the cemetery. She really didn't want to go. The thought of her baby's lifeless body in a casket in the ground made her shudder.

God, go before me this day.

She got out of bed, took a shower and dressed for the day. Reading a note from her aunt saying she'd already left for Jerry's, Ava grabbed a banana and a bottle of water, gathered up the decorations and headed out the door.

Parking near her family's plots, she frowned when she saw Holden's truck. *God, I really don't know if I'm up to this.* She rubbed her temples, then gathered up her strength. *No more running.*

She scooped up the flowers and flags and walked to the plot. For a moment, she faltered when she saw Holden kneeling on one knee, with one hand resting flat against their baby's marker. He must have heard her approaching because he turned, and she saw a look of sadness in his eyes before it quickly changed to anger.

Lifting her chin and sucking in a deep breath, she walked the rest of the way. "Hello, Holden."

He narrowed his gaze. "What are you doing here?"

His tone sent a tremor of fury through her. He had every right to be upset with her that she hadn't been honest in the beginning, but that did not negate the loss she had experienced. "I have every right to visit my son, too," she snapped.

His eyes widened in surprise, then narrowed again. "You said you don't like to come."

Her ire faded as she placed the decorations on the markers, being sure to arrange them as Aunt Irene would have. "I don't." She wiped her forehead with her palm. "I try not to remember him here."

"It's the only place I have to remember him."

Holden's words stabbed her heart. She had felt their baby move in her womb. Believed he was healthy and growing. After the ultrasound and the diagnosis, she'd been numb. Paralyzed with questions and fear, believing God had punished her or that she had done something wrong. When he'd stopped kicking, and another ultrasound confirmed he'd died, the doctor had induced her, and she'd labored for hours for her baby who never took a breath. Her fingers instinctively pressed against her stomach. She held tight to the memories of his active kicks in the womb. "I really am sorry, Holden."

He opened his arms wide. "I would have taken care of you, would have done everything in my power to help our baby survive, to make him well."

She shook her head as she dug a pen and a piece of paper out of her purse. She wrote down the word that would be forever imprinted on her heart, then shoved the paper into his hand. "This is what he had. Look it up. You couldn't fix him."

He frowned at the sheet of paper. "What does this even say?"

"Anencephaly. He was missing most of his brain."

Holden wrinkled his nose and his chin quivered. "But surely doctors can... Medicine is so advanced nowadays and..."

"It happens soon after conception. There was nothing you could do."

His eyes flashed with renewed anger. "I could have known."

"Yes." She lifted her purse strap higher on her shoulder. "And you should have." She turned to walk back to her car, then stopped. "Aunt Irene was with me when he was born. We knew he was already dead—" her voice caught and she swallowed back her emotions "—but she brought a camera and took lots of pictures. You can see them anytime you'd like."

Ava took a step, then a hand grabbed her and turned her around. Strong arms enfolded her and held her tight. She leaned against Holden and wrapped her arms around his waist. After a few moments, without a word, he released her and walked to his truck.

She waited until he'd driven away before kneeling next to the marker. Allowing her fingers to gently trace the letter *H,* she whispered, "Your daddy would have loved you so much." She pressed a kiss to her fingertips, then touched the letter before walking back to the car.

Aunt Irene had returned home from Jerry's by the time Ava arrived. She smiled at her aunt, determined to have a good holiday with her family. "How was practice?"

"Terrific. We're ready. How was the decorating?" Her aunt pretended to sound nonchalant, but Ava knew the woman too well. She worried about Ava.

"It looks nice. What can I do to help?" She decided not to mention seeing Holden. Today was not a day to worry about what was past. It was a day to celebrate freedom and those who'd fought so diligently for it.

Aunt Irene gave her a bunch of celery and Ava pulled off the stalks and washed them in the sink. The phone rang, and Aunt Irene answered. Her expression fell, then she said goodbye and hung up.

"What was that about?" asked Ava.

"Seems we'll be one person shy tonight for dinner." Aunt Irene waved and forced a smile. "That's all right, though. One less mouth to feed."

"Who's not coming?"

Her aunt averted her gaze. "Holden's gonna spend the holiday with Jake's family."

Holden sat beside Traci and Carl in the performing arts center at the high school. Dad had been a nervous wreck most of the morning about Senior Idol having finally arrived. Daryl and Sara stood in the door, and he waved for them to join the group. Ava followed, and Holden's heart constricted. She was so pretty in a white sundress and blue jewelry. Her skin glowed from the hot Arizona sun. She'd pulled her hair back in a low ponytail, making her look younger and reminding him of the summer they'd fallen in love.

Sara plopped down beside their sister and rubbed Traci's belly. She leaned down. "How's our little sunflower doing today?"

Traci touched her slightly bulging belly. "Growing like a weed. According to the book, she's about eleven inches long and weighs a pound."

Carl lifted his finger and nodded. "And we go by the book."

Traci punched his arm. "Don't make fun of me."

Sara punched him, as well. "Yeah. We're excited about our little girl." She cooed at Traci's belly. "Aren't we, little one?"

Carl raised his hands in surrender. "I'm just kidding. I can't wait to see her. And just so you know, she's gonna be a daddy's girl."

Holden bit his tongue as his sisters and brothers-in-law continued to banter. He was excited to have a niece and wanted her to be healthy, and yet a piece of him was envious of them because his son hadn't been. Out of the corner of his eye, he noticed Ava was studying the program a bit too intensely.

He'd researched the word *anencephaly*. Looked at pictures. Read stories. Researched causes and cures. Ava hadn't done anything to cause their son's deformity, but she'd been able to feel their son move inside her. He would have wanted to touch her belly, to feel proof of little Holden's life when he was safe inside his mother. Instead, he could only visit a marker in a cemetery and see pictures he hadn't yet had the courage to ask for.

The coordinator for the senior center walked onto the stage. "Good afternoon, family and friends. We are pleased to have you with us this afternoon." She talked about the center's activities and funds needed to help keep it running. She even showed a quick slideshow of pictures from the last year. Holden rubbed his eyes with his knuckle. He hadn't been sleeping well.

The show finally started with a ventriloquist act. The older gentleman told terrific jokes, but most of the time he forgot to move the puppet's mouth when the little guy was supposed to be talking. The next performance was a trio of ladies singing a patriotic song. Holden bowed his head and prayed for strength not to cover his ears. Afterward, a married couple waltzed, then a man sang. Next, a woman read some of her own poetry, and on and on.

The coordinator's voice boomed over the microphone. "Our next performance is Irene Hall and Jerry Whitaker singing 'Islands in the Stream,' originally sung by Dolly Parton and Kenny Rogers."

The family clapped, and Holden let out a loud whistle. His dad and Irene walked onto the stage holding hands. He wore a black Western shirt with white trim, blue jeans, a black belt with a large red buckle, black boots and a black cowboy hat with red trim. But Irene was a hoot. She wore a huge blond wig, a red-and-white-checkered scarf around her neck and red cowgirl boots. The Western-style dress matched the scarf and even included the enhancements Dolly Parton was known for.

Holden glanced at Ava, who tried to cover her giggles with the program in front of her mouth. He hadn't realized Phoebe sat beside her. She pointed to her chest and mouthed, "I made the dress. You like it?"

He nodded and winked as he gave her a thumbs-up. The music started, and Holden noticed his dad looked paler than he should have. Irene grabbed his hand, and his dad started to sing. Whispers sounded around them from people who were surprised that Jerry Whitaker had such a nice voice.

Irene belted her lyrics, and someone in the corner whistled. She had such an amazing talent. They started their choreography of simple moves that went along with the words of the song. His dad's face shone with adoration as he looked into Irene's eyes as he sang.

When the song ended, the crowd jumped out of their seats and applauded. Dad and Irene bowed, and she blew kisses to the crowd. The show soon ended and the winner was announced. The ventriloquist. They hadn't expected Dad and Irene to win. Once a winner, no longer a participant.

The crowd started to leave, and Holden and the family stood up and waited for Dad and Irene to make their way to them.

"They did a terrific job," said Sara.

Daryl added, "I never knew ol' Jerry had it in him."

"None of us did," said Traci. "And to think Irene said he used to sing when they were in high school."

"I didn't see Mitch and Matt," said Sara.

Ava pointed to the other side of the hall, where they were beginning to make their way toward them. "They came in a little late."

Dad and Irene finally made it past the crowd of friends congratulating them. Their faces shone with delight, and they still held hands. Irene gestured toward all of them. "Let's get some ice cream together."

"Sounds good to me and little squirt," said Traci, as she rubbed her belly.

"She's our sunflower," reprimanded Sara.

Daryl patted Dad's back. "I still can't believe you can sing."

"Wonders never cease." His voice slurred the *S*.

Irene frowned. "Jerry, are you okay?"

He swatted the air. "I'm fine. I've never sung in front of a group like that. Just got a little nervous."

Irene didn't seem convinced, but Dad kissed her cheek and she perked up and clapped her hands. "Let's get that ice cream."

Holden followed his family to the parking lot. He felt sure it wouldn't be long before his dad and Irene announced their engagement. Everyone around him had found love, while he'd only found out painful secrets.

Chapter 19

A noise startled Ava from her sleep. She squinted and rubbed her eyes with her fingertips. It was still dark. She glanced at the alarm clock. One o'clock. She heard the noise again. She blinked several times. *That's my phone. Who would possibly be calling at this hour?*

She reached for the smartphone, pulled it off the charger and pressed Talk. "Hello?"

"Ava. It's Holden."

The panic in his voice startled her. She sat up straight. "Holden, what's wrong?"

"It's Dad. We're at the hospital. He's had a stroke."

"What?" Her heartbeat raced and a cold sweat washed down her body.

"He's gonna be okay, but he wants Irene."

Ava nodded, then realized he couldn't see her response. "Okay. We'll be right there."

Ava pressed End and flung her legs over the side of the

bed. She looked up, startled, when she saw her aunt standing in the door. Fear filled Aunt Irene's expression and she gripped her nightgown at her chest. "Who was that?"

"It was Holden."

"What's wrong with Jerry?" Her voice sounded frail.

Ava went to her aunt and grabbed her hands. "Holden said he's had a stroke, but that he's going to be okay. He wants to see you."

Aunt Irene gasped, then turned on her heels. "Let's get ready quick."

Ava threw on a pair of capris and a thin T-shirt. She brushed her teeth, then combed her hair and put it in a ponytail. After tossing some fruit, granola bars and bottles of water into a bag, she scooped up her purse and dug out her keys. "I'm ready, Aunt Irene."

Her aunt raced out of the bedroom with her shirt half tucked in her pants, and wearing mismatched shoes. Ava pointed to her feet, and she raced back into the bedroom and switched them, then shooed Ava out the door.

"Please, God. Heal his body," Irene prayed.

Ava drove as quickly as she could, and dropped her aunt off at the entrance, then parked the car. Her mind swirled with prayers. For Jerry to be okay. For her aunt to be calm. For Holden to be strong. For Holden's sisters and brothers-in-law. *Comfort them all, Lord.*

She walked into the emergency room lobby and saw Holden sitting in a chair. He was leaning forward with his elbows resting on his knees and his hands cupping his head. She bit her lip, unsure what to do. She didn't see his sisters or Aunt Irene. Daryl stood by a vending machine, while Carl slouched in a chair, fast asleep, his head pressed back against the wall.

Holden already reeled from the hurt of finding out about their son, and she constantly prayed for him to find peace and forgiveness. Seeing him hurt anew over his dad made her heart clench, and Ava couldn't help but move toward him and sit down.

He glanced at her. His eyelids were heavy with fatigue and worry. Then he dipped his head again. Ava swallowed. She wanted to reach over and touch his shoulder or his arm, but she didn't want to make him angry. She was probably the last person he wanted to console him.

Pushing the insecurity away, she looped her hand around his arm. She opened her mouth to share sympathy or a prayer or just a word of concern. Then she snapped her lips shut. He didn't need words right now.

They sat there for several moments, while Holden leaned forward, his head in his hands. One of Ava's hands wrapped around his elbow, and she tucked the other between her knees to keep it from shaking.

"He went to bed early. Said he had a headache." Holden's words were quiet, and he didn't lift his head. "I don't even know why, but I went in to check on him." He lifted his head and looked at her. "I never do that. For some reason, I just went in there."

"The Holy Spirit nudged you." Ava bit her lip. She meant to only listen.

Holden studied her before he nodded. "Yeah. I think so, too." He touched his cheek. "Dad's face was pulled down on the side, and he could hardly lift his arms. I called 911, and Dad whispered, "Aspirin.""

Ava wanted to squeeze Holden's biceps or fold her arms around him, something to show him that she was there to comfort him.

"I gave him the aspirin. Had to put it in his mouth, and he fought to swallow." Holden grinned. "He's a stubborn fighter, you know."

Ava allowed a slow smile. She knew. Holden was the

same way. When he decided something, he had a one-track mind about it. He'd tried to talk to her all those years ago. Now, she prayed he wouldn't remain zeroed in on not forgiving her.

He shook his head. "Dad scared the life out of me, but the doc thinks he's gonna be okay."

"Holden." Traci's voice sounded behind them.

He turned. "Yeah?"

"Dad's resting. I'm gonna go home so I can work in the morning." She pointed to the doors. "You can go back there with Irene and Sara and sit with him."

"Sure."

Without saying a word to Ava, Holden stood and walked through the doors. Her heart broke that he didn't want her with him. She could be a comfort for him to lean on. She thought of Holden's words at the cemetery and how stricken he'd looked that she hadn't allowed him to help her through the pain. She'd been such a fool. She hadn't protected him. She'd taken away his chance to mourn and her chance for comfort. She couldn't blame him if he never forgave her.

Holden was pleased with his dad's progress. In only a week's time, he was able to get around with a walker, and a lot of the drooping of his face had gone away. His speech was till slurred, but it was understandable.

And yet Dad struggled with depression and fear. He had moments when he would panic and want Holden and both of his sisters near him. Dad would grab a notepad and pen to be sure he could scribble words. His writing looked like that of a kindergartener, but as long as he could get a word or two out he was satisfied.

Holden walked to the barn to take care of a few chores. He was glad to be away from the tension for a while. The hot sun beat down upon him. He'd need to check on the cattle, as well.

Once Holden finished all the work he could, he walked back to the house. He smiled when he saw Jake and several of the boys standing around his father. Dad's grin was still a bit lopsided as he pointed to the papers in his hand. "They brought cards."

Zack saw Holden and gave him a quick hug. "We missed you last night."

Holden tousled the redhead's hair. "I missed you guys, too. I should be there next week."

"We're glad your dad's okay. We prayed for him last night," said Vince.

Holden patted Jake's new stepson's back. "I appreciate that."

"Why don't you boys get ice cream?" said Dad as he pointed toward the kitchen. Each word was a battle, but he'd gotten them out. The boys scurried inside, proof enough that they'd understood.

Sara's voice came from the kitchen. "We've got ice cream sandwiches, but you'll have to eat them in here."

Chair legs clanked against the floor as the boys sat down at the table. Holden gave his dad a thumbs-up. "That'll keep 'em busy for a few minutes."

His dad smiled a lopsided smile again, then leaned back in the chair, clasped his hands together and closed his eyes. He'd been up awhile when Holden went out to check on the ranch, so he was certainly ready for a nap now.

"Megan's bringing over some supper tomorrow night. Irene already told her what she could make," said Jake.

Holden glanced to the woman who stood at their kitchen sink, washing dishes. She had spent a good deal of the morning chopping vegetables and fruits into pieces Dad could eat. She watched over him like Betty did her own calf.

Holden shook his friend's hand. "We appreciate that. Irene would never admit it, but she probably needs a break."

"Does Ava come over, too?"

He shrugged. "Sometimes."

"How are the two of you?"

"Fine, I suppose. I make myself scarce when she comes. It's not like I don't have plenty to do."

"Still not talking to her then?"

Holden lifted one shoulder. "We've talked. I just don't go out of my way...."

"You're just being stubborn."

"No." He tapped his chest with his finger. "I think I have good reason to be angry."

Jake lifted his arms. "So, you're going to stay mad forever? What good will that do? What will it prove?"

"It doesn't have to prove anything."

"You're hurting yourself. Forgive her and move on."

"I'm trying to forgive her," Holden exclaimed.

Dad stirred. He opened his eyes, looked around, then shut them again.

"Everything all right in there?" Irene asked.

Holden's cheeks warmed. He didn't want her to know what they were talking about. "It's fine. Sorry 'bout that."

Jake rubbed his palms together and looked past him. "Listen, Holden. We can talk about this another time."

"No. You listen. Just because you forgive someone doesn't mean you want to have a relationship with them."

Jake closed his eyes and exhaled, then tipped his head for Holden to look behind him. He turned and saw Ava standing there with a package of bottled water.

Feeling like a complete idiot, he grabbed the package from her hands, but not before noting the sadness that flicked through her gaze.

She gestured toward the front door. "I…I have some more groceries in the car."

Jake nodded. "The boys and I will help."

Holden put the water in the kitchen and instructed the kids to help Jake with the groceries. He brushed past his sister out the back door and into his truck. He rolled down the windows. The air was hot and sticky, but he relished the heat against his face as he drove away.

He didn't know where he wanted to go. He just needed to leave. Ava had returned to Surprise back in the spring, and Holden had hoped for a chance with her again. Had got his heart all set on love. Jess was getting married. Jake had already tied the knot. Dad and Irene might as well be hitched. Then Holden had found out about the baby, and Dad had had a stroke. Holden punched the seat beside him. A man could take only so much.

He found himself parked outside the physical therapy clinic. He and Ava had fallen in love with each other again starting right there, of all places. He wasn't lying when he'd told her she was a good therapist. She'd grown up so much since he'd known her eight years ago. Grew up for the better, and he'd found that he loved her all the more.

And yet each time he looked at her now he saw the lie. Not an outright lie, but one of omission. A secret she should have shared. Forgive her, Jake said, as if Holden didn't know he should forgive her. But knowing what to do and being able to do it were two different things.

He stared out the windshield at the purples and pinks surrounding the setting sun, and remembered their time together watching the movie at the stadium. *God, I don't want to feel this way. I want to forgive her. I just don't know how.*

Chapter 20

By the end of a miserably hot August, Ava's hope that Holden would someday forgive her waned. With ninety degree and higher temperatures at night, she often woke up in a sweat, which then led to her fretting over Holden's words to Jake more than a month ago. *Just because you forgive someone doesn't mean you want a relationship with them.*

With the words fresh in her mind again in the wee hours of the morning, Ava made her way to the bathroom and splashed cold water on her face. She settled into the wingback chair in her bedroom and lifted the Bible off the end table. In the past, she'd used her electronic device to read scriptures. Lately, she'd wanted to touch the words on the page and mark her thoughts and questions.

She looked at the verses she'd read the day before. Many people quoted the Romans verse in their times of trouble, but for years she'd fought the words Paul had penned. Closing her eyes, she whispered the passage imprinted on her heart.

"'We know that all things work together for good for those who love God, who are called according to His purpose.'"

But how could her baby's death work good? And what about bad choices? She and Holden had been Christians that night all those years ago. They knew they'd gone against God's plan for them. Every decision in life resulted in a consequence, good or bad. She mumbled the words again. "'All things.'"

Because of that night, a child had been formed. Though he hadn't taken a breath, she'd felt his life within her. Had it not been for her son, she might have pursued her parents' life, one of caring only for career and getting ahead. And from her baby's death, she had learned to cling to God for comfort and peace. She'd meet precious baby Holden one day in Glory.

She flipped the pages of the Bible to the front and traced Holden's name and date of birth and death with her fingertips. Indescribable pain had come from his death, and yet good had indeed come as well.

She opened the table drawer and pulled out the small photo album. She didn't often look through the pictures Aunt Irene had taken of Holden, because Ava basked in remembering him alive in her womb. Opening to the first page, she studied his perfect face. The nurse had placed a blue cap on his head, covering the exposed brain. His eyes bulged a bit, but his cheeks were chubby, his little mouth perfect and shaped like his daddy's. In the picture, she held him in her arms, with tears streaking down her cheeks.

Again, her heart broke that she hadn't told Holden. When the doctor had explained the diagnosis, and that her son would certainly die after birth, if not before, she couldn't see the benefit of telling him. She hadn't talked to Holden in months. He didn't know she was pregnant. Why call him to come see a dead baby?

She traced their child's small, perfectly formed hands in the picture. She hadn't realized how good it would be to hold her son. In her eyes, he wasn't deformed. He was perfect, and he'd left her to live in the arms of Jesus. Somehow holding him had allowed her to release him.

And she'd stolen that opportunity from Holden.

She put the photo album away. The past couldn't be undone, and consequences did result from all actions. Holden might never be able to forgive her in a way that allowed them to have a relationship again. The thought pained her, but she had to choose to find the good in it.

She stood up and changed into some comfortable, cool clothes, then brushed her hair and pulled it back into a ponytail. When she walked into the kitchen, Aunt Irene was pouring a glass of orange juice. Ava glanced at the clock. She hadn't realized she'd spent so long reading the Bible, praying and looking at pictures.

"You ready to work on the garden?" asked her aunt.

"Absolutely, though I am not sure how you will be able to keep up with all the vegetables you're planting at Jerry and Holden's house."

"I thought you loved to garden."

Ava took a glass from the cabinet and poured herself some juice. "I do, but I don't live at their house. Making sure all those vegetables are taken care of will be a chore."

"Jerry will help. And Holden."

Ava unwrapped a granola bar. "Holden is busy on the ranch, and Jerry is doing great, but…"

"Are you saying broccoli, cucumbers, cabbage, carrots, snap beans, green onions, spinach and turnips sound like a lot of veggies to keep track of?" Aunt Irene smiled.

Ava lifted her finger. "And don't forget we planted sweet corn seeds last month."

She snapped her fingers. "That we did." She winked.

"You might just have to quit your day job and move over there."

Ava laughed. "First of all, I love my day job. And secondly, I think Holden would have a few things to say about that."

Aunt Irene shrugged. "I don't know. I think he's coming around. It's just taking him a while. Quite a shock, you know."

Ava picked at her fingernail. "I was so wrong not to tell him."

"You can't change what's done. You've asked for forgiveness." Her aunt patted her hand. "You can only focus on following God's will now."

"I know." Ava swallowed the last of her juice, then placed the glass in the sink. "We better get over there. The longer we wait, the hotter it's gonna be."

Aunt Irene walked down the hall. "Let me get my shoes, and we'll go."

Ava opened the door to see the sun just peeking up over the horizon. The sky, a mixture of purples, pinks and yellows, seemed to beckon the city to wake up and enjoy a new day. Ava would dig into the earth, literally, allowing God's nature to be a balm to her heart and soul. No matter what happened with Holden, she would trust the Lord.

Holden dreaded the weekends. Saturdays and Sundays meant a lot of time spent with Ava. Irene came to the house every day to help Dad, and his recovery had been incredible. Already, he got around without a walker and talked without problems. He still napped a lot and battled fear that he'd lose the ability to communicate again, but overall, his health was terrific.

Holden set bowls of hot whole-grain cereal on the kitchen table. Dad cut up bananas and placed the pieces on a saucer while Holden grabbed an orange for himself. They sat at the table, and his dad offered a quick blessing.

"Ava's planting again today." Jerry popped a bite of banana in his mouth and chewed.

"I know." Holden nodded toward his cereal. "As soon as I finish breakfast, I'll look in on the cattle, check the fences."

"Gonna avoid the house all day, huh?"

"No. I've just got things to do."

"Mmm-hmm."

Dad took a bite of cereal. He spent a lot longer chewing his food. He seemed to exaggerate each bite to insure his jaws still worked as they should.

"How are you feeling today, Dad?"

"Good." A shadow washed across his features. "The physical rehabilitation has been a lot easier than the emotional."

He held up a bottle of pills. "I never dreamed I'd take medicine for anxiety. Always prided myself on giving my troubles over to God."

Holden shifted in his chair. He'd been struggling in his quiet moments with the Lord. Every lesson he taught the boys at church and every scripture he read seemed to focus on forgiveness and love.

Love wasn't the problem. He'd given up trying to overcome the feelings he had for Ava. Each time he saw her, his heart drummed to a disjointed, staccato beat that took his breath away. But his feelings were more than just emotion. He loved her. Wanted the best for her. Yet he couldn't get past the truth that she hadn't trusted him enough to tell him about their baby. He felt betrayed by her.

His dad tapped the top of the medicine bottle, drawing Holden from his thoughts. "But God is using this medicine to help me. Pride's a funny thing." He chuckled. "I believed my way of thinking was right. Showed faith." He tapped his chest. "But it was my way. God uses all kinds of things to draw us near. This helps clear my mind so that I can lean on Him."

The front door opened. Irene walked into the kitchen, then leaned down and pressed a kiss on Dad's cheek. She grinned at Holden. "How are two of my favorite guys this morning?"

"Good," said Holden.

"Ava didn't come with you?" asked Dad. "I thought you had gardening in mind."

Irene pointed to the yard. "She's already hard at work. That girl sure loves to garden. Was up well before sunrise."

"She was?" said Dad.

"She might have had a few other things on her mind. That one's not been sleeping too good lately." She patted Dad's back, then pointed to Holden. "Before you set out to do your chores, I wondered if you'd help me a minute."

Holden stood. "Of course."

He followed her into the spare bedroom, where she had him move the dresser and nightstand. They seemed fine where they'd been before, but Irene had been so helpful and kind he decided not to argue. She plopped down on the foot of the bed, then tapped the mattress beside her. "I'd like to talk with you a minute, if you don't mind."

Holden's stomach tightened when he sat down and she pulled a small blue photo album out of the bag. He knew what was inside that book. Part of him wanted to run out of the door. Ava had offered to let him see pictures, but he'd never been able to conjure the courage to ask. He feared what his son would look like, feared what he'd feel when he saw the baby.

She placed her hand on top of the album, then looked at Holden. "Do you know Ava rarely sleeps? Her faith has grown tremendously, but she still hurts that she never told you about your son."

Holden tried to harden his heart against the words, but the sincerity in Irene's gaze weakened his resolve. "She's apologized. I know she meant it."

"No, Holden. I don't think you do. She was shocked when she learned of the baby. Soon after, she was told he wouldn't live, possibly not even take a single breath. She was only eighteen."

Holden stared at the album in Irene's grasp. He wanted to see, yet he didn't.

"In her mind, she couldn't see the good in calling you after months of being gone, to tell you she was pregnant, and that your baby was going to die." Irene placed her hand on his shoulder. "She thought she was protecting you."

Holden opened his mouth to respond, but Irene shook her head. "Then she saw him, and she knew she'd been wrong."

Irene opened the book, and Holden bit his bottom lip as he looked down at his son in Ava's arms. Irene placed the book in his hands, then walked out of the bedroom and shut the door. Holden sat there and devoured each page. With his little blue cap on his head, the child looked like a perfect, alive baby.

Holden flipped through the pages and stopped at one of Ava holding their son. Her profile showed tears streaming down her cheek as she touched their child's lips with her finger. Beneath the picture she'd written, "Daddy's mouth."

Holden's heart broke, and the Holy Spirit slipped in a peace he couldn't explain or comprehend. He'd forgiven her.

Chapter 21

Ava sat down at the table for the now-weekly Sunday dinner with her cousins and Holden's family. For the last month Holden had sat beside Traci and Carl, but to her surprise, he took a seat beside her today. He pointed to the salad on his plate. "Looks delicious."

"Thanks." Ava's cheeks warmed, as that was the first time he'd spoken to her without a reason in two months.

The families passed around the food, then Jerry prayed over their meal. For the first time, Matt had brought a girlfriend, a petite brunette named April. He smiled at her constantly, and she blushed with each word he spoke to her. Despite the crowded room, Mitch and Ellie whispered and giggled intimately, and Ava wondered how long it would be before her older cousins announced engagements. Traci and Carl and Sara and Daryl bantered back and forth about the baby, then sports, then the baby.

"Ha!" Sara crowed at something Traci had said. "At least Dad's name is still up for grabs."

Traci bobbed her head. "Maybe we'll just name our little girl Jerry. The name can go both ways."

Sara pointed at her sister. "No. The agreement is the first grand*son* will be named after Dad. You can't go changing the rules just because you're having a girl."

Traci huffed as she folded her hands over her bulging belly. "You sound like you're not happy to have a niece."

Sara leaned over and rubbed Traci's belly. "Don't you listen to Mama, little girl. You know Aunt Sara will be your favorite." She sat up. "But you know, now Daryl and I will most likely have the first boy."

"Wait a minute," Daryl said. "No babies yet."

Sara shrugged. "At least we know Holden's not having the first grandson. Doesn't even have a girlfriend."

Everyone stopped talking at Sara's words. Keeping her gaze down, Ava picked up her glass and took a slow drink of tea. She then took a bite of grilled salmon, praying the families would start talking again.

She hadn't known the Whitaker children had made a deal to name the firstborn grandson after Jerry. She'd named her son after Holden. Her baby could have been Jerry's namesake, and yet she was glad he shared his own father's name.

When Daryl asked Mitch what he thought about the Surprise Saguaros upcoming baseball season, Ava breathed a sigh of relief.

"So, how have you been, Ava?" Holden whispered beside her.

She looked down at her plate. Each night she prayed Holden would forgive her and talk to her again, but guilt welled inside her at the question. "I'm fine."

"Thanks for working on the garden. It looks great."

"You're welcome. I just hate that it will mean more work for you, since I'll be at the clinic during the week."

He waved a hand. "It's worth the extra work. Dad needs the fresh veggies."

She glanced at him, and he smiled at her. The sincerity in his gaze sent a shiver through her, and her heartbeat quickened. She cleared her throat. "How have you been?"

He pursed his lips. "Thinking. Praying."

Ava opened her mouth to apologize again, just as Jerry and Aunt Irene stood up at the end of the table. Jerry looped his arm around her aunt's. He was continuing to recover well from the stroke, and though he wasn't working on the ranch, he'd been able to fix odds and ends in the house and do some small jobs in the barn.

He lifted his free hand now. "Irene and I have an announcement to make."

Sara grabbed Daryl's hand, while Carl wrapped his arm around Traci's back. Pleasure laced the expressions of both families, as they assumed the two were about to announce an upcoming wedding. They were blessed that both families appeared eager for the union.

Jerry nodded to her aunt. "You go ahead and tell them."

Aunt Irene smiled as she dipped her chin and lifted her shoulders like a young teenager telling her family about her new boyfriend. "Jerry and I are getting married."

Cheers of joy and clapping sounded around the table, and Holden whistled in approval.

Jerry lifted his hand again. "Next Saturday."

Silence fell over the room. Sara shook her head, then leaned closer. "What?"

Aunt Irene giggled. "We're getting married on Saturday."

Traci frowned as she rubbed her belly. "No wedding? Well, okay. We thought…"

"No. We're having a wedding," said Aunt Irene.

Ava furrowed her brows. How did her aunt plan to pull this off? There would be so much to do.

"Phoebe's already agreed to fix food. I already ordered a cake." She motioned around the room. "'Course, it'll only be us—" she tapped her lips "—and maybe a few friends, since we're going to have the wedding here."

Holden pointed to the table. "Here? We're having it here?"

"Sure," said Jerry. "You and I will get the place ready. Clear out the living room furniture. Fix up a few decorations." He kissed Aunt Irene's cheek. "She'll tell us what she wants."

Ava looked at Holden's shocked expression. She knew he was in for a challenging and exhausting week.

"And Ava and I will take care of everything else," said Aunt Irene.

Ava glanced at Holden again. A mischievous smile lifted his lips. "You're in for a fun week."

"Sounds like you are, too."

Holden frowned suddenly as he looked back at Aunt Irene and his dad. "Wait a minute. I guess we're moving Irene's stuff, as well?"

Ava's jaw dropped. She hadn't thought of that. Aunt Irene would probably want to sell her home. Ava hadn't even thought of looking at apartments or houses yet. She and her aunt got along well, and they'd been so busy.

"No," said Jerry. "I'm moving over there."

"What?" said Holden. "You love the ranch."

Jerry shook his head. "I'm never going to be able to work the place like I used to. It's time to settle down." He scratched his jaw. "I was planning to sit down with you tonight and figure it all out."

Ava's mind whirled. She couldn't live with Aunt Irene and Jerry. They'd be newlyweds. They'd want to have time to themselves. Now, she was in an even greater predicament. She needed to get out. And fast.

Holden knew the wedding was going to be a bigger deal than Dad and Irene said. He carried in four more folding chairs and set them down in the cleared out living room. Ava groaned as she tied yet another oversize ribbon on the back of a chair. He chuckled. "I'm not done yet."

She snarled at him. "I'm aware of that."

He laughed as he walked outside to get more chairs from the truck. The week had been busy and exhausting as Irene added decorations and guests to the ceremony. Someone in her Sunday school class had introduced her to a website filled with wedding ideas, and Irene attempted to use more than half of them. At least that's how it seemed to Holden.

He had to admit the fake trees she'd had at her house did look nice standing on each side of the large window in the center of the living room. He'd strung Christmas lights through the limbs, and Ava had tied small golden bows to several branches.

"We're heading into our golden years together, so we're having a golden wedding," Irene had proclaimed last week.

She'd bought stars cut out of thick cardboard, and he and Ava spent an evening spray painting them gold. When they'd dried, the two of them had hung the stars from the ceiling with thin gold ribbons. They'd painted mason jars gold and stuck single white flowers inside and set them on pedestals he'd made with dowel rods and pieces of wood cut into circles.

Setting down the last of the folding chairs, he surveyed the room. The window and the trees made a beautiful, yet simple focal point. The stars looked nice, and the flower-filled mason jars and pedestals lining the walls on either side, plus the thick ribbon around the chairs, transformed the living room into a golden celebration.

He bent down beside Ava. "Want some help?"

She nodded. "I think my fingers are gonna fall off."

"We can't have that. You've gotta help Phoebe set out food, then help your aunt get ready, then—"

She blew a strand of hair out of her face. "And at some point I'm gonna have to try to make myself presentable."

The strand fell again, and he brushed it away from her eyes. "You're already beautiful, Ava."

He cupped her chin when her gaze fell to his mouth. He wanted to kiss her again, to wrap his arms around her and tell her how much he loved her, that he'd forgiven her. Dipping his chin, he lowered his face toward her.

"Ava, can you come here a minute?" her aunt called from the back bedroom.

Holden straightened up and dropped his hand from her face. "I can finish in here."

He watched as Ava walked down the hall to the spare room, where Irene was getting ready. In only a few hours, their guests would arrive. Some fifty of them. So much for "only family and a few friends."

He finished the bows, then headed into the kitchen to check on Phoebe and a few of Irene's friends from church. "How's the food coming, ladies?"

"Wonderfully," said Phoebe, "but could you get the vegetables from the refrigerator in the garage? We'll need to cut those up and set them on platters pretty soon."

He got the vegetables and put them on the table for Phoebe, then checked the thermostat and turned the air conditioner down a few degrees. The temperature was still well over a hundred the first week of September, and they'd deal with a lot of body heat with so many people in the house.

"Dad." He walked into his father's bedroom. "How're you doin'? Need anything?"

Decked out in a cream-colored suit and gold tie, his father stood in front of the dresser mirror looking at himself from various angles. He clicked his tongue. "Not something I'd normally pick out."

Holden grinned. No. His dad preferred jeans and an old plaid shirt. "It's definitely on the modern side."

"You sayin' I look like a girl?"

Holden lifted his hands. "No. I'm saying you look hip."

Dad huffed, then curled his lips into a grin. "I suppose I don't care what I look like if it's what Irene wants." He picked up the boutonniere, a white rose with petals that had been dipped in gold paint. "Will you put this on me?"

"Sure." Holden pinned the flower. "Irene's really good to you."

"She is at that." He narrowed his gaze. "Her niece would be a pretty good catch, as well."

Holden nodded. "I've always thought so."

Dad lifted his chin and raised his eyebrows. "And you think so again?"

"Yep."

His father scratched his jaw. "So when I get back from my honeymoon, I might have some new news to think about."

Holden chuckled as he shrugged. "I don't know, Dad. We'll see."

"Humph." He studied him, then motioned him toward the door. "You better go on and get ready. We don't have much longer now."

Since his dad had asked him to be the best man, Irene had picked out an outfit for him, as well. He dressed in the cream-colored shirt and khakis, then fixed the gold tie around his neck.

When he walked out of the bedroom, he saw Ava making her way down the hall to Irene's room. She wore a shimmery gold sundress that hung from her shoulders like a perfect waterfall. A gold bow tied in the front of her waist accentuated her thin shape.

She bit her lip and stopped when she saw him. "Here." A blush spread across her cheeks when she reached up and fixed his collar.

He took her hand in his and stared into blue eyes that shimmered with gold around the corners. "Wow."

She swallowed, and he felt a slight tremble in her hand. She averted her gaze. "You look very handsome, Holden."

"Ava—"

"Ava, I need your help again," said her aunt.

"I'm coming." She pulled away and walked into the bedroom.

He would talk to her. Tonight.

Chapter 22

Ava flopped onto the recliner that Holden had moved to the patio for the wedding. The last of the wedding guests had finally left, and Jerry and Aunt Irene were on their way to their honeymoon. Traci and Sara and their husbands were still cleaning the kitchen, but after taking off ribbons and folding up fifty chairs, Ava didn't have the energy to help.

Holden stepped onto the patio. "What are you doing? Bumming out on us?"

Ava dropped her head back on the leather cushion and closed her eyes. "Call me whatever you want. I'm not moving from this chair."

He laughed, a hearty, good-natured sound that made her smile. She drank in the masculine sight of him. He'd taken off the atrocious gold tie Aunt Irene had picked out, and undone the top two buttons. His sleeves were rolled up to his elbows, as she would have expected. Surprisingly, he hadn't changed from the khaki pants to his Wrangler jeans, but he still looked unbelievably handsome.

He stuck out his bottom lip. "I was hoping you'd take a ride with me."

Ava studied the man she loved with every beat of her heart. The past week had been wonderful. They'd had a good time doing Aunt Irene's bidding, be it paint, move, arrange or fix whatever she dreamed up for them to do. He'd been kind and helpful. In only a week's time, something had changed, and she knew he'd forgiven her.

She leaned forward and released an exaggerated sigh. "I suppose you've twisted my arm. I guess I'll go with you."

Before she realized what he was doing, Holden lifted her into his arms. On impulse, she wrapped hers around his neck, and her heart pounded at his closeness. He carried her to his truck and set her in the cab, and her cheeks warmed as she chuckled, "Holden, I don't even have my shoes."

His face was so close to hers she thought he might kiss her, as he had the night they'd watched the movie. Instead, he lifted a finger. "Be right back."

While he ran into the house, she took several breaths, then peeked at her reflection in the visor mirror. She licked her finger and rubbed away some of the mascara smudges from when she'd gotten teary-eyed during the wedding ceremony.

He walked back outside with her shoes and purse in his hands, and she flipped the visor up in a hurry. When he got inside, she asked, "So, where are we going?"

"It's a surprise."

She pointed to the cowboy hat on his head, then raised her eyebrows.

He shrugged. "I feel naked without my hat."

Ava laughed as Holden drove down the road. Though the sun had set, the air was still hot and muggy. She didn't care as she rolled down the window and let the heat whip through her hair.

Realizing they were headed to the White Tank Mountains, Ava rubbed her hands together and stared out the window at the passing desert filled with cacti and creosote bushes.

He parked and she waited until he walked around the front of the truck, opened the door and took her hand to help her down. He didn't let go of her, and she relished the feel of his coarse, strong skin against hers. She didn't say a word as he guided her to their favorite trail. For a moment, she was eighteen, following the love of her life wherever he wanted her to go. At twenty-six, and with more experience behind her, she loved the man with a deeper bond than she'd known those eight years ago.

A crescent moon and stars dotted the dark night sky. He stopped at their favorite spot and took both her hands in his. "I love you, Ava."

Tears welled in her eyes, and her chin quivered. Holden never minced words. He spoke his mind, plain and simple. "I love you, too, Holden."

He wrapped his arms around her and pressed her face against his chest. The tears streamed down her cheeks. "I'm sorry, Holden."

She felt his kisses on the top of her head. "I forgive you."

He cupped her cheeks and kissed her forehead, then the tip of her nose, then her mouth. Ava's toes curled with the kiss and she reached up and raked her fingers through his hair.

He growled as he pulled away from her, then knelt down on one knee. Ava brushed the tears off her cheeks as he drew the black box out of his pocket. "Marry me."

She jumped toward him, wrapping her arms around his neck. "Absolutely, yes."

He harrumphed, but stayed upright as she pressed her

lips against his again. He broke away from her. "You're killin' me, woman."

She bit her lip and giggled as he slipped the ring on her finger. Still holding her hand, he said, "How long of an engagement are you thinking?"

Ava shook her head. "Holden, I don't want a big wedding. Really. I'm with Jake and Megan. Let's just go to the courthouse."

Holden's lips lifted in a slow smile. "I'd like to see you all dolled up in a pretty dress, but…" He paused, and she lifted her brows. "What do you say we get married here?"

"Holden, that would be wonderful."

"Next week."

Ava blinked. "What?"

He shrugged, and the glimmer in his eye seemed more mischievous by the second. "I already reserved a spot."

She opened her mouth, then swatted his shoulder. "And what if I say no to such a quick date?"

"Then I'll cancel." He pulled her close. "But I hope you won't. After all, next week you're gonna need a place to stay. Unless you want to live with your aunt and my dad. And I really could use a little help with that garden."

She placed her hand on her hip. "Are you trying to blackmail me?"

He shook his head, then kissed her hand. "I'm trying to marry you."

She bit her bottom lip as butterflies swarmed in her belly. The idea of being married in only a week's time sounded…wonderful. "Yes. Let's do it."

Holden held Ava's hands and drank in her beauty on their wedding day. She wore a gorgeous ivory dress with thin straps around her shoulders. The soft fabric started as a V below her neck, then crisscrossed to her waist. A belt of lace with a flower that looked like an ivory poppy wrapped around her waist. The bottom of the dress flowed in layers that looked like an upside-down tulip. Holding a bouquet of purple lupines and yellow poppies, she was a beautiful desert bride for a rugged Arizona cowboy.

Their pastor spoke of charity from the Bible. He talked about Jesus's love for his church and how Holden was to love Ava with the same intensity. Holden caressed her hands with his thumbs, inwardly promising God to do just that.

"Do you, Holden Whitaker, take this woman to be your lawfully wedded wife, promising to love her through joy and sorrow, sickness and health, as long as you both shall live?" asked their pastor.

"I do."

A slight blush darkened Ava's cheeks, and Holden's gaze devoured every nuance of her face. Her bright blue eyes with a darker shade of blue around the pupils. The small freckle to the side of her left eye. Her nose, the perfect length and width for her face. Her thin lips spread into a smile exposing straight white teeth.

The pastor continued, "Do you, Ava Herbert, take this man to be your lawfully wedded husband, promising to love him through joy and sorrow, sickness and health, as long as you both shall live?"

She squeezed his hands gently. "I do."

The pastor turned toward Dad, who smiled at Holden as he gave him the ring. Holden placed the ring on the tip of Ava's finger. "With this ring, I promise to love you and cherish you for the rest of my life." He slipped the white gold all the way down her finger.

She turned, took his ring from her aunt Irene and placed it against his fingertip. "I love you, Holden. With this ring, I promise to love you and cherish you and trust you." She leaned forward and whispered, "No more running." She smiled as she finished, "For the rest of my life."

Holden's heart flipped in his chest, and he ached to take her in his arms and kiss her until his lips fell off.

The pastor began, "By the power vested in me by the state of Arizona, I now pronounce you…"

Holden couldn't wait. He pulled Ava toward him and pressed his lips to hers. She giggled as she cupped his cheeks with her hands. Her fingernails scratched his jaw ever so slightly, and Holden growled as he lifted her off her feet. Ava squealed, then started to laugh. "What are you doing?"

"You're my wife now. We're heading out of here."

"Holden." His new stepmother fanned her face. "At least let us all give her a hug."

He looked at their guests, his sisters and their husbands and Ava's cousins and their girlfriends. Her parents had chosen not to come. Though Ava's bosses had been disappointed, she'd been determined to have a very small ceremony. No reception. Her aunt Irene, his new stepmother, had arranged a little reception for their families after the wedding, but Holden and Ava wouldn't be there. They'd already be on their way to their honeymoon.

He placed her on her feet. "Oh, all right."

Ava punched his arm. "Holden, you're an overgrown brute."

He kissed her forehead. "An overgrown brute who's in love with his wife."

While the family gave Ava hugs and warm wishes, Holden shook his dad's hand. His father patted his shoulder, then gave him a hug. "I'm happy for you, son. She's a good woman, and you'll be a fine husband."

"Thanks, Dad."

"I've never told you this, because I knew God had to be the One to work on your heart." Jerry raked his fingers through his graying hair. "Your mom wanted me to forgive her for leaving. Wanted to come back home when you were just a little thing. I was too proud. Wouldn't even consider it."

Holden watched as his dad rubbed the back of his neck. "A week later she died." He looked up, and Holden saw the torture in his expression. "I'm not saying my forgiveness would have changed her death. Our lives are in God's hands." He pointed to his chest. "But forgiveness would have changed me." He spread his arms. "God forgave me all my sins. He requires me to forgive others, and my pride kept me from doing that when your mother was still alive."

Holden allowed his dad's words to seep into his heart. He looked at his beautiful wife. If he'd allowed anger, pride and bitterness to take root, he wouldn't have her as his bride today. He hugged his dad. "Thanks for sharing with me."

Dad patted his back again. "Now go get your bride."

Holden didn't need any additional encouragement. He swept Ava off her feet again and shook his head at his family. "Sorry, y'all, but this woman is going with me."

She waved over his shoulder as he walked toward the truck. Before he put her down in the cab, she pressed her palms against his cheeks, making his lips smash together like a duck. She kissed them and said, "I love you, Holden Whitaker."

"I love you, Ava Whitaker."

Epilogue

One year later

Ava gripped the sides of the hospital bed and pushed with every ounce of strength she could muster. On the doctor's count, she blew out short puffs of air, then pushed again.

"He's crowning," the doctor announced.

Holden pressed his forehead against hers. "You're doing so good, Ava. So, so good."

"Let's go again," said the doctor.

Ava took Holden's strong hand and squeezed as she bore down again. She stopped and breathed a quick prayer for God to help her get her son out. Once again, she pushed.

"His head is out. Just one more push."

Ava clenched her jaw and bore down with all that was in her. A cry sounded, and Ava's body trembled with joy.

Holden cupped his mouth as he looked at their son.

"Time to cut the cord, Holden," the nurse announced.

Holden cut the cord, then kissed Ava's forehead before walking to the other side of the room with their baby.

Her doctor tapped her knee and smiled at her. His kind eyes told her he knew what she needed to hear. "He looks perfect, Ava." He motioned behind him. "And those wails sound good."

Sudden sobs wrenched from within in her as she praised God for blessing her with another son. The nurse handed her tissues and rubbed Ava's arm. "It's okay to cry."

Ava nodded as she allowed sorrow and joy and fear and thanksgiving to flow out of her. Within moments, Holden brought their son to her and laid him on her chest. "Jerry's all cleaned up and ready to see Mommy."

She grinned that Holden had beaten his sisters at having the first grandson. Their boy wore a small blue cap just like their first son, and Ava took it off him. She needed to see his perfect head, had to feel his downy skin. He blinked, then stared at her as if to say, "So that's what you look like." Touching his lips with her fingertips, she looked up at her husband. "He has your lips, just like his brother."

Holden's eyes glistened with tears as he bent down and kissed her head. "He's the most amazing thing I've ever seen. You did good." He touched their son's cheek with his fingertip. "And it wasn't nearly as bad as I thought."

Ava turned her head and glared at him. "If I could get out of this bed…"

Holden burst out laughing. When she saw that the doctor and nurse also narrowed their gazes at him, she chuckled. "I might not have to get up. They might get you for me."

The pediatric nurse stood beside the bed. "We need to take him back and get him all checked out for you."

Ava reluctantly nodded as the woman replaced the little cap and took Jerry from her arms.

Holden squeezed her shoulder. "I'll make sure they don't hurt him."

She shook her head as Holden followed the nurse and their baby. He was going to be a terrific dad, just as he'd always be her Arizona cowboy.

* * * * *

REQUEST YOUR FREE BOOKS!

2 FREE INSPIRATIONAL NOVELS
PLUS 2
FREE
MYSTERY GIFTS

Love Inspired

YES! Please send me 2 FREE Love Inspired® novels and my 2 FREE mystery gifts (gifts are worth about $10). After receiving them, if I don't wish to receive any more books, I can return the shipping statement marked "cancel." If I don't cancel, I will receive 6 brand-new novels every month and be billed just $4.74 per book in the U.S. or $5.24 per book in Canada. That's a savings of at least 21% off the cover price. It's quite a bargain! Shipping and handling is just 50¢ per book in the U.S. and 75¢ per book in Canada.* I understand that accepting the 2 free books and gifts places me under no obligation to buy anything. I can always return a shipment and cancel at any time. Even if I never buy another book, the two free books and gifts are mine to keep forever.

105/305 IDN F49N

Name _____ (PLEASE PRINT)

Address _____ Apt. #

City _____ State/Prov. _____ Zip/Postal Code

Signature (if under 18, a parent or guardian must sign)

Mail to the Harlequin® Reader Service:
IN U.S.A.: P.O. Box 1867, Buffalo, NY 14240-1867
IN CANADA: P.O. Box 609, Fort Erie, Ontario L2A 5X3

**Are you a subscriber to Love Inspired books
and want to receive the larger-print edition?
Call 1-800-873-8635 or visit www.ReaderService.com.**

* Terms and prices subject to change without notice. Prices do not include applicable taxes. Sales tax applicable in N.Y. Canadian residents will be charged applicable taxes. Offer not valid in Quebec. This offer is limited to one order per household. Not valid for current subscribers to Love Inspired books. All orders subject to credit approval. Credit or debit balances in a customer's account(s) may be offset by any other outstanding balance owed by or to the customer. Please allow 4 to 6 weeks for delivery. Offer available while quantities last.

Your Privacy—The Harlequin® Reader Service is committed to protecting your privacy. Our Privacy Policy is available online at www.ReaderService.com or upon request from the Harlequin Reader Service.
We make a portion of our mailing list available to reputable third parties that offer products we believe may interest you. If you prefer that we not exchange your name with third parties, or if you wish to clarify or modify your communication preferences, please visit us at www.ReaderService.com/consumerschoice or write to us at Harlequin Reader Service Preference Service, P.O. Box 9062, Buffalo, NY 14269. Include your complete name and address.

LIDIR13R

REQUEST YOUR FREE BOOKS!

2 FREE INSPIRATIONAL NOVELS
PLUS 2
FREE
MYSTERY GIFTS

Love Inspired
HISTORICAL
INSPIRATIONAL HISTORICAL ROMANCE

REQUEST YOUR FREE BOOKS!
2 FREE RIVETING INSPIRATIONAL NOVELS
PLUS 2 FREE MYSTERY GIFTS

Love Inspired®
SUSPENSE

YES! Please send me 2 FREE Love Inspired® Suspense novels and my 2 FREE mystery gifts (gifts are worth about $10). After receiving them, if I don't wish to receive any more books, I can return the shipping statement marked "cancel." If I don't cancel, I will receive 4 brand-new novels every month and be billed just $4.74 per book in the U.S. or $5.24 per book in Canada. That's a savings of at least 21% off the cover price. It's quite a bargain! Shipping and handling is just 50¢ per book in the U.S. and 75¢ per book in Canada.* I understand that accepting the 2 free books and gifts places me under no obligation to buy anything. I can always return a shipment and cancel at any time. Even if I never buy another book, the two free books and gifts are mine to keep forever.

123/323 IDN F5AN

Name	(PLEASE PRINT)	
Address		Apt. #
City	State/Prov.	Zip/Postal Code

Signature (if under 18, a parent or guardian must sign)

Mail to the Harlequin® Reader Service:
IN U.S.A.: P.O. Box 1867, Buffalo, NY 14240-1867
IN CANADA: P.O. Box 609, Fort Erie, Ontario L2A 5X3

**Are you a current subscriber to Love Inspired Suspense books and want to receive the larger-print edition?
Call 1-800-873-8635 or visit www.ReaderService.com.**

* Terms and prices subject to change without notice. Prices do not include applicable taxes. Sales tax applicable in N.Y. Canadian residents will be charged applicable taxes. Offer not valid in Quebec. This offer is limited to one order per household. Not valid for current subscribers to Love Inspired Suspense books. All orders subject to credit approval. Credit or debit balances in a customer's account(s) may be offset by any other outstanding balance owed by or to the customer. Please allow 4 to 6 weeks for delivery. Offer available while quantities last.

LISDIR13R

REQUEST YOUR FREE BOOKS!
2 FREE WHOLESOME ROMANCE NOVELS
IN LARGER PRINT
PLUS 2
FREE
MYSTERY GIFTS

❋❋❋❋❋❋❋❋❋❋❋❋❋❋❋❋❋❋❋❋

HEARTWARMING™

❄❄❄❄❄❄❄❄❄❄❄❄❄❄❄❄❄❄❄❄

Wholesome, tender romances

YES! Please send me 2 FREE Harlequin® Heartwarming Larger-Print novels and my 2 FREE mystery gifts (gifts worth about $10). After receiving them, if I don't wish to receive any more books, I can return the shipping statement marked "cancel." If I don't cancel, I will receive 4 brand-new larger-print novels every month and be billed just $4.99 per book in the U.S. or $5.74 per book in Canada. That's a savings of at least 23% off the cover price. It's quite a bargain! Shipping and handling is just 50¢ per book in the U.S. and 75¢ per book in Canada.* I understand that accepting the 2 free books and gifts places me under no obligation to buy anything. I can always return a shipment and cancel at any time. Even if I never buy another book, the two free books and gifts are mine to keep forever.

161/361 IDN F47N

Name	(PLEASE PRINT)	
Address		Apt. #
City	State/Prov.	Zip/Postal Code

Signature (if under 18, a parent or guardian must sign)

Mail to the **Harlequin®** Reader Service:
IN U.S.A.: P.O. Box 1867, Buffalo, NY 14240-1867
IN CANADA: P.O. Box 609, Fort Erie, Ontario L2A 5X3

* Terms and prices subject to change without notice. Prices do not include applicable taxes. Sales tax applicable in N.Y. Canadian residents will be charged applicable taxes. Offer not valid in Quebec. This offer is limited to one order per household. Not valid for current subscribers to Harlequin Heartwarming larger-print books. All orders subject to credit approval. Credit or debit balances in a customer's account(s) may be offset by any other outstanding balance owed by or to the customer. Please allow 4 to 6 weeks for delivery. Offer available while quantities last.

Your Privacy—The Harlequin® Reader Service is committed to protecting your privacy. Our Privacy Policy is available online at www.ReaderService.com or upon request from the Harlequin Reader Service.

We make a portion of our mailing list available to reputable third parties that offer products we believe may interest you. If you prefer that we not exchange your name with third parties, or if you wish to clarify or modify your communication preferences, please visit us at www.ReaderService.com/consumerschoice or write to us at Harlequin Reader Service Preference Service, P.O. Box 9062, Buffalo, NY 14269. Include your complete name and address.

HWDIR13R

ReaderService.com

Manage your account online!

- Review your order history
- Manage your payments
- Update your address

> ### *We've designed the Harlequin® Reader Service website just for you.*

Enjoy all the features!

- Reader excerpts from any series
- Respond to mailings and special monthly offers
- Discover new series available to you
- Browse the Bonus Bucks catalog
- Share your feedback

Visit us at:

ReaderService.com